The Last Spike

1906

CY WARMAN

TABLE OF CONTENTS

THE LAST SPIKE	5
THE BELLE OF ATHABASCA	17
PATHFINDING IN THE NORTHWEST	23
THE CURÉ'S CHRISTMAS GIFT	27
CHASING THE WHITE MAIL	45
OPPRESSING THE OPPRESSOR	49
THE IRON HORSE AND THE TROLLEY	55
IN THE BLACK CAÑON	61
JACK RAMSEY'S REASON	67
THE GREAT WRECK ON THE PÈRE MARQUETTE	73
THE STORY OF AN ENGLISHMAN	79
ON THE LIMITED	85
THE CONQUEST OF ALASKA	89
NUMBER THREE	97
THE STUFF THAT STANDS	103
THE MILWAUKEE RUN	111

THE LAST SPIKE

I.

"Then there is nothing against him but his poverty?"

"And general appearance."

"He's the handsomest man in America."

"Yes, that is against him, and the fact that he is always in America. He appears to be afraid to get out."

"He's the bravest boy in the world," she replied, her face still to the window. "He risked his life to drag me from under the ice," she added, with a girl's loyalty to her hero and a woman's pride in the man she loves.

"Well, I must own he has nerve," her father added, "or he never would have accepted my conditions."

"And what where these conditions, pray?" the young woman asked, turning and facing her father, who sat watching her every move and gesture.

"First of all, he must do something; and do it off his own bat. His old father spent his last dollar to educate this young rascal, to equip him for the battle of life, and his sole achievement is a curve that nobody can find. Now I insist he shall do something, and I have given him five years for the work."

"Five years!" she gasped, as she lost herself in a big chair.

"He is to have time to forget you, and you are to have ample opportunity to forget him, which you will doubtless do, for you are not to meet or communicate with each other during this period of probation."

"Did he promise this?"

"Upon his honor."

"And if he break that promise?"

"Ah, then he would be without honor, and you would not marry him." A moment's silence followed, broken by a long, deep sigh that ended in little quivering waves, like the faint ripples that reach the shore,—the whispered echoes of the sobbing sea.

"O father, it is cruel! cruel! cruel!" she cried, raising a tearful face to him.

"It is justice, stern justice; to you, my dear, to myself, and this fine young fellow who has stolen your heart. Let him show himself worthy of you, and you have my blessing and my fortune."

"Is he going soon?"

"He is gone."

The young woman knelt by her father's chair and bowed her head upon his knee, quivering with grief.

This stern man, who had humped himself and made a million, put a hand on her head and said:

"Ma-Mary"—and then choked up.

II

The tent boy put a small white card down on General Dodge's desk one morning, upon which was printed:

J. Bradford, C.E.

The General, who was at that time chief engineer in charge of the construction of the first Pacific Railroad, turned the bit of pasteboard over. It seemed so short and simple. He ran his eyes over a printed list, alphabetically arranged, of directors, promoters, statesmen, capitalists, and others who were in the habit of signing "letters of recommendation" for young men who wanted to do something and begin well up the ladder.

There were no Bradfords. Burgess and Blodgett were the only B's, and the General was glad. His desk was constantly littered with the "letters" of tenderfeet, and his office-tent filled with their portmanteaus, holding dress suits and fine linen.

Here was a curiosity—a man with no press notices, no character, only one initial and two chasers.

"Show him in," said the General, addressing the one luxury his hogan held. A few moments later the chief engineer was looking into the eye of a young man, who returned the look and asked frankly, and without embarrassment, for work with the engineers.

"Impossible, young man—full up," was the brief answer.

"Now," thought the General, "he'll begin to beat his breast and haul out his 'pull.'" The young man only smiled sadly, and said, "I'm sorry. I saw an 'ad' for men in the Bee yesterday, and hoped to be in time," he added, rising.

"Men! Yes, we want men to drive mules and stakes, to grade, lay track, and fight Indians—but engineers? We've got 'em to use for cross-ties."

"I am able and willing to do any of these things—except the Indians—and I'll tackle that if nothing else offers."

"There's a man for you," said the General to his assistant as Bradford went out with a note to Jack Casement, who was handling the graders, teamsters, and Indian fighters. "No influential friends, no baggage, no character, just a man, able to stand alone—a real man in corduroys and flannels."

Coming up to the gang, Bradford singled out the man who was swearing loudest and delivered the note. "Fall in," said the straw boss, and Bradford got busy. He could handle one end of a thirty-foot rail with ease, and before night, without exciting the other workmen or making any show of superiority, he had quietly, almost unconsciously, become the leader of the track-laying gang. The foreman called Casement's attention to the new man, and Casement watched him for five minutes.

Two days later a big teamster, having found a bottle of fire-water, became separated from his reasoning faculties, crowded under an old dump-cart, and fell asleep.

"Say, young fellow," said the foreman, panting up the grade to where Bradford was placing a rail, "can you skin mules?"

"I can drive a team, if that's what you mean," was the reply.

"How many?"

"Well," said Bradford, with his quiet smile, "when I was a boy I used to drive six on the Montpelier stage."

So he took the eight-mule team and amazed the multitude by hauling heavier loads than any other team, because he knew how to handle his whip and lines, and because he was careful and determined to succeed. Whatever he did he did it with both hands, backed up by all the enthusiasm of youth and the unconscious strength of an absolutely faultless physique, and directed by a remarkably clear brain. When the timekeeper got killed, Bradford took his place, for he could "read writin'," an accomplishment rare among the laborers. When the bookkeeper got drunk he kept the books, working overtime at night.

In the rush and roar of the fight General Dodge had forgotten the young man in corduroys until General Casement called his attention to the young man's work. The engineers wanted Bradford, and Casement had kicked, and, fearing defeat, had appealed to the chief. They sent for Bradford. Yes, he was an engineer, he said, and when he said it they knew it was true. He was quite willing to remain in the store department until he could be relieved, but, naturally, he would prefer field work.

He got it, and at once. Also, he got some Indian fighting. In less than a year he was assigned to the task of locating a section of the line west of the Platte. Coming in on a construction train to make his first report, the train was held up, robbed, and burned by a band of Sioux. Bradford and the train crew were rescued by General Dodge himself, who happened to be following them with his "arsenal" car, and who heard at Plumb Creek of the fight and of the last stand that Bradford and his handful of men were making in the way car, which they had detached and pushed back from the burning train. Such cool heroism as Bradford displayed here could not escape the notice of so trained an Indian fighter as General Dodge. Bradford was not only complimented, but was invited into the General's private car. The General's admiration for the young pathfinder grew as he received a detailed and comprehensive report of the work being done out on the pathless plains. He knew the worth of this work, because he knew the country, for he had spent whole months together exploring it while in command of that territory, where he had been purposely placed by General Sherman, without whose encouragement the West could not have been known at that time, and without whose help as commander-in-chief of the United States army the road could not have been built.

As the pathfinders neared the Rockies the troops had to guard them constantly. The engineers reconnoitered, surveyed, located, and built inside the picket lines. The men marched to work to the tap of the drum, stacked arms on the dump, and were ready at a moment's notice to fall in and fight. Many of the graders were old soldiers, and a little fight only rested them. Indeed there was more military air about this work than had been or has since been about the building of a railroad in this country. It was one big battle, from the first stake west of Omaha to the last spike at Promontory—a battle that lasted five long years; and if the men had marked the graves of those who fell in that fierce fight their monuments, properly distributed, might have served as mile-posts on the great overland route to-day. But the mounds were unmarked, most of them, and many there were who had no mounds, and whose home names were never known even to their comrades. If this thing had been done on British soil, and all the heroic deeds had been recorded and rewarded, a small foundry could have been kept busy beating out V.C.'s. They could not know, these silent heroes fighting far out in the wilderness, what a glorious country they were conquering—what an empire they were opening for all the people of the land. Occasionally there came to the men at the front old, worn newspapers, telling wild stories of the failure of the enterprise. At other times they heard of changes in the Board of Directors, the election of a new President, tales of jobs and looting, but they concerned themselves only with the work in hand. No breath of scandal ever reached these pioneer trail-makers, or, if it did, it failed to find a lodging-place, but blew by. Ample opportunity they had to plunder, to sell supplies to the Indians or the Mormons, but no one of the men who did the actual work of bridging the continent has ever been accused of a selfish or dishonest act.

During his second winter of service Bradford slept away out in the Rockies, studying the snowslides and drifts. For three winters they did this, and in summer they set stakes, keeping one eye out for Indians and the other for wash-outs, and when, after untold hardships, privation, and youth-destroying labor, they had located a piece of road, out of the path of the slide and the washout, a well-groomed son of a politician would come up from the Capital, and, in the capacity of Government expert, condemn it all. Then strong men would eat their whiskers and the weaker ones would grow blasphemous and curse the country that afforded no facilities for sorrow-drowning.

Once, at the end of a long, hard winter, when spring and the Sioux came, they found Bradford and a handful of helpers just breaking camp in a sheltered hollow in the hills. Hiding in the crags, the warriors waited until Bradford went out alone to try to shoot a deer, and incidentally to sound a drift, and then they surrounded him. He fought until his gun was unloaded, and then emptied his revolver; but ever dodging and crouching from tree to rock, the red men, whose country he and his companions had invaded, came nearer and nearer. In a little while the fight was hand to hand. There was not the faintest show for escape; to be taken alive was to be tortured to death, so he fought on, clubbing his revolver until a well-directed blow from a war club caught the gun, sent it whirling through the top of a nearby cedar, and left the pathfinder empty-handed. The chief sprang forward and lifted his hatchet that had caused more than one paleface to bite the dust. For the faintest fraction of a second it stood poised above Bradford's head, then out shot the engineer's strong right arm, and the Indian lay flat six feet away.

For a moment the warriors seemed helpless with mingled awe and admiration, but when Bradford stooped to grab his empty rifle they came out of their trance. A dull blow, a sense of whirling round swiftly, a sudden sunset, stars—darkness, and all pain had gone!

III

When Bradford came to they were fixing him for the fun. His back was against a tree, his feet pinioned, and his elbows held secure by a rawhide rope. He knew what it meant. He knew by the look of joy on the freshly smeared faces at his waking, by the pitch-pine wood that had been brought up, and by the fagots at his feet. The big chief who had felt his fist came up, grinning, and jabbed a buckhorn cactus against the engineer's thigh, and when the latter tried to move out of reach they all grunted and danced with delight. They had been uneasy lest the white man might not wake.

The sun, sailing westward in a burnished sea of blue, seemed to stand still for a moment and then dropped down behind the range, as if to escape from the hellish scene. The shadows served only to increase the gloom in the heart of the captive. Glancing over his shoulder toward the east, he observed that his captors had brought him down near to the edge of the plain. Having satisfied themselves that their victim had plenty of life left in him, the Indians began to arrange the fuel. With the return of consciousness came an inexpressible longing to live. Suddenly his iron will asserted itself, and appealing to his great strength, surged until the rawhide ropes were buried in his flesh. Not for a moment while he stood on his feet and fought them on the morning of that day had hope entirely deserted him. Four years of hardship, of privation, and adventure had so strengthened his courage that to give up was to die.

Presently, when he had exhausted his strength and sat quietly, the Indians went on with the preliminaries. The gold in the west grew deeper, the shadows in the foothills darker, as the moments sped. Swiftly the captive's mind ran over the events of the past four years. This was his first failure, and this was the end of it all—of the years of working and waiting.

Clenching his fists, he lifted his hot face to the dumb sky, but no sound escaped from his parched and parted lips. Suddenly a light shone on the semicircle of feather-framed faces in front of him, and he heard the familiar crackling of burning boughs. Glancing toward the ground he saw that the fagots were on fire. He felt the hot breath of flame, and then for the first time realized what torture meant. Again he surged, and surged again, the cedars crackled, the red fiends danced. Another effort, the rawhide parted and he stood erect. With both hands freed he felt new strength, new hope. He tried to free himself from the pyre, but his feet were fettered, and he fell among his captors. Two or three of them seized him, but he shook them off and stood up again.

But it was useless. From every side the Indians rushed upon him and bore him to the ground. Still he fought and struggled, and as he fought the air seemed full of strange, wild sounds, of shouts and shots and hoof-beating on the dry, hard earth. He seemed to see, as through a veil, scores of Indians, Indians afoot and on horseback, naked Indians and Indians in soldier clothes. Once he thought he saw a white face gleam just as he got to his feet, but at that moment the big chief stood before him, his battle-axe uplifted. The engineer's head was whirling. Instinctively he tried to use the strong right arm, but it had lost its cunning. The roar of battle grew apace, the axe descended, the left arm went up and took the blow of the handle, but the edge of the weapon reached over and split the white man's chin. As he fell heavily to the earth the light went out again.

Save for the stars that stood above him it was still dark when Bradford woke. He felt blankets beneath him, and asked in a whisper: "Who's here?"

"Major North, me call him," said the Pawnee scout, who was watching over the wounded man.

A moment later the gallant Major was leaning over Bradford, encouraging him, assuring him that he was all right, but warning him of the danger of making the least bit of noise.

IV

With all his strength and pluck, it took time for Bradford to recuperate. His next work was in Washington, where, with notes and maps, his strong personality and logical arguments, he caused the Government to overrule an expert who wanted to change an important piece of road, and who had arbitrarily fixed the meeting of the mountains and plains far up in the foothills.[1]

When Bradford returned to the West he found that the whole country had suddenly taken a great and growing interest in the transcontinental line. Many of the leading newspapers had dug up their old war correspondents and sent them out to the front.

These gifted prevaricators found the plain, unvarnished story of each day's work as much as they cared to send in at night, for the builders were now putting down four and five miles of road every working day. Such road building the world had never seen, and news of it now ran round the earth. At night these tireless story-tellers listened to the strange tales told by the trail-makers, then stole away to their tents and wrote them out for the people at home, while the heroes of the stories slept.

The track-layers were now climbing up over the crest of the continent, the locaters were dropping down the Pacific slope, with the prowling pathfinders peeping over into the Utah Valley. Before the road reached Salt Lake City the builders were made aware of the presence, power, and opposition of Brigham Young. The head of the church had decreed that the road must pass to the south of the lake, and as the Central Pacific had surveyed a line that way, and General Dodge had declared in favor of the northern route, the Mormons threw their powerful influence to the Southern. The Union Pacific was boycotted, and all good Mormons forbidden to aid the road in any way.

Here, again, the chief engineer brought Bradford's diplomacy to bear on Brigham and won him over.

While the Union Pacific was building west, the Central Pacific had been building east, and here, in the Salt Lake basin, the advance forces of the two companies met. The United States Congress directed that the rails should be joined wherever the two came together, but the bonus ($32,000 to the mile) left a good margin to the builders in the valley, so, instead of joining the rails, the pathfinders only said "Howdy do!" and then "Good-bye!" and kept going. The graders followed close upon the heels of the engineers, so that by the time the track-layers met the two grades paralleled each other for a distance of two hundred miles. When the rails actually met, the Government compelled the two roads to couple up. It had been a friendly contest that left no bad blood. Indeed they were all willing to stop, for the iron trail was open from the Atlantic to the Pacific.

V

The tenth day of May, 1869, was the date fixed for the driving of the last spike and the official opening of the line. Special trains, carrying prominent railway and Government officials, were hurrying out from the East, while up from the Golden Gate came another train bringing the flower of 'Frisco to witness, and some of them to take an active part in, the celebration. The day was like twenty-nine other May days that month in the Salt Lake Valley, fair and warm, but with a cool breeze blowing over the sagebrush. The dusty army of trail-makers had been resting for two days, waiting for the people to come in clean store clothes, to make speeches, to eat and drink, and drive the golden spike. Some Chinese laborers had opened a temporary laundry near the camp, and were coining money washing faded blue overalls for their white comrades. Many of the engineers and foremen had dressed up that morning, and a few had fished out a white shirt. Judah and Strawbridge, of the Central, had little chips of straw hats that had been harvested in the summer of '65. Here and there you saw a sombrero, the wide hat of the cowboy, and the big, soft, shapeless head cover of the Mormon, with a little bunch of whiskers on his chin. General Dodge came from his arsenal car, that stood on an improvised spur, in a bright, new uniform. Of the special trains, that of Governor Stanford was first to arrive, with its straight-stacked locomotive and Celestial servants. Then the U.P. engine panted up, with its burnished bands and balloon stack, that reminded you of the skirts the women wore, save that it funnelled down. When the ladies began to jump down, the cayuses of the cowboys began to snort and side-step, for they had seen nothing like these tents the women stood up in.

Elaborate arrangements had been made for transmitting the news of the celebration to the world. All the important telegraph offices of the country were connected with Promontory, Utah, that day, so that the blow of the hammer driving the last spike was communicated by the click of the instrument to every office reached by the wires. From the Atlantic to the Pacific the people were rejoicing and celebrating the event, but the worn heroes who had dreamed it over and over for five years, while they lay in their blankets with only the dry, hard earth beneath them, seemed unable to realize that the work was really done and that they could now go home, those who had homes to go to, eat soft bread, and sleep between sheets.

Out under an awning, made by stretching a blanket between a couple of dump-carts, Bradford lay, reading a 'Frisco paper that had come by Governor Stanford's special; but even that failed to hold his thoughts. His heart was away out on the Atlantic coast, and he would be hurrying that way on the morrow, the guest of the chief engineer. He had lost his mother when a boy, and his father just a year previous to his banishment, but he had never lost faith in the one woman he had loved, and he had loved her all his life, for they had been playmates. Now all this fuss about driving the last spike was of no importance to him. The one thing he longed for, lived for, was to get back to "God's country." He heard the speeches by Governor Stanford for the Central, and General Dodge for the Union Pacific; heard the prayer offered up by the Rev. Dr. Todd, of Pittsfield; heard the General dictate to the operator:

"All ready," and presently the operator sang out the reply from the far East:

"All ready here!" and then the silver hammer began beating the golden spike into the laurel tie, which bore a silver plate, upon which was engraved:

"The Last Tie
Laid in the Completion of the Pacific
Railroads.
May 10, 1869."

After the ceremony there was handshaking among the men and some kissing among the women, as the two parties—one from either coast—mingled, and then the General's tent boy came under the blanket to call Bradford, for the General wanted him at once. Somehow Bradford's mind flew back to his first meeting with this boy. He caught the boy by the arms, held him off, and looked at him. "Say, boy," he asked, "have I changed as much as you have? Why, only the other day you were a freckled beauty in high-water trousers. You're a man now, with whiskers and a busted lip. Say, have I changed, too?"

"Naw; you're just the same," said the boy. "Come now, the Gen's waitin'."

"Judge Manning," said General Dodge, in his strong, clear voice, "you have been calling us 'heroes'; now I want to introduce the one hero of all this heroic band—the man who has given of muscle and brain all that a magnificent and brilliant young man could give, and who deserves the first place on the roll of honor among the great engineers of our time."

As the General pronounced the Judge's name Bradford involuntarily clenched his fists and stepped back. The Judge turned slowly, looking all the while at the General, thrilled by his eloquent earnestness, and catching something of the General's admiration for so eminent a man.

"Mr. Bradford," the General concluded, "this is Judge Manning, of Boston, who came to our rescue financially and helped us to complete this great work to which you have so bravely and loyally contributed."

"Mr. Bradford, did you say?"

"Well, yes. He's only Jim Bradford out here, where we are in a hurry, but he'll be Mr. Bradford in Boston, and the biggest man in town when he gets back."

All nervousness had gone from Bradford, and he looked steadily into the strong face before him.

"Jim Bradford," the millionnaire repeated, still holding the engineer's hand.

"Yes, Judge Manning, I'm Jim Bradford," said the bearded pathfinder, trying to smile and appear natural.

Suddenly realizing that some explanation was due the General, the Judge turned and said, but without releasing the engineer's hand: "Why, I know this young man—knew his father. We were friends from boyhood."

Slowly he returned his glance to Bradford. "Will you come into my car in an hour from now?" he asked.

"Thank you," said Bradford, nodding, and with a quick, simultaneous pressure of hands, the two men parted.

VI

Bradford has often since felt grateful to the Judge for that five years' sentence, but never has he forgotten the happy thought that prompted the capitalist to give him this last hour, in which to get into a fresh suit and have his beard trimmed. Bradford wore a beard always now, not because a handsome beard makes a handsome man handsomer, but because it covered and hid the hideous scar in his chin that had been carved there by the Sioux chief.

When the black porter bowed and showed Bradford into Mr. Manning's private car, the pleasure of their late meeting and the Judge's kindly greeting vanished instantly. It was all submerged and swept away, obliterated and forgotten in the great wave of inexpressible joy that now filled and thrilled his throbbing heart, for it was Mary Manning who came forward to greet him. For nearly an hour she and her father had been listening to the wonderful story of the last five years of the engineer's life. When the wily General caught the drift of the young lady's mind, and had been informed of the conditional engagement of the young people, he left nothing unsaid that would add to the fame and glory of the trail-maker. With radiant face she heard of his heroism, tireless industry, and wonderful engineering feats; but when the narrator came to tell how he had been captured and held and tortured by the Indians, she slipped her trembling hand into the hand of her father, and when he saw her hot tears falling he lifted the hand and kissed it, leaving upon it tears of his own.

The Judge now produced his cigar case, and the General, bowing to the young lady, followed the great financier to the other end of the car, leaving Mary alone, for they had seen Bradford coming up the track.

The dew of her sweet sorrow was still upon her face when Bradford entered, but the sunshine of her smile soon dried it up. The hands he reached for escaped him. They were about his face; then their great joy and the tears it brought blinded them, and the wild beating of their happy hearts drowned their voices so that they could neither see nor hear, and neither has ever been able to say just what happened.

On the day following this happy meeting, when the consolidated special was rolling east-ward, while the Judge and the General smoked in the latter's car, the tent boy brought a telegram back to the happy pair. It was delivered to Miss Manning, and she read it aloud:

"Washington, May 11, 1869.

"General G.M. Dodge:

"In common with millions I sat yesterday and heard the mystic taps of the telegraph battery announce the nailing of the last spike in the Great Pacific Road. All honor to you, to Durant, to Jack and Dan Casement, to Reed and the thousands of brave followers who have wrought out this glorious problem, spite of changes, storms, and even doubts of the incredulous, and all the obstacles you have now happily surmounted!

"W.T. Sherman,

"General."

"Well!" she exclaimed, letting her hands and the telegram fall in her lap, "he doesn't even mention my hero."

"Oh, yes, he does, my dear," said Bradford, laughing. "I'm one of the 'thousands of brave followers.'"

Then they both laughed and forgot it, for they were too happy to bother with trifles.

FOOTNOTES

[1] The subsidy from the Government was $16,000 a mile on the plains, and $48,000 a mile in the mountains.

THE BELLE OF ATHABASCA

Athabasca Belle did not burst upon Smith the Silent all at once, like a rainbow or a sunrise in the desert. He would never say she had been thrust upon him. She was acquired, he said, in an unguarded moment.

The trouble began when Smith was pathfinding on the upper Athabasca for the new transcontinental. Among his other assets Smith had two camp kettles. One was marked with the three initials of the new line, which, at that time, existed only on writing material, empty pots, and equally empty parliamentary perorations. The other was not marked at all. It was the personal property of Jaquis, who cooked for Smith and his outfit. The Belle was a fine looking Cree—tall, strong, magnifique. Jaquis warmed to her from the start, but the Belle was not for Jaquis, himself a Siwash three to one. She scarcely looked at him, and answered him only when he asked if she'd encore the pork and beans. But she looked at Smith. She would sit by the hour, her elbow on her knee and her chin in her hand, watching him wistfully, while he drew crazy, crooked lines or pictured mountains with rivers running between them—all of which, from the Belle's point of view, was not only a waste of time, but had absolutely nothing to do with the case.

The Belle and her brown mother came to the camp of the Silent first one glorious morn in the moon of August, with a basket of wild berries and a pair of beaded moccasins. Smith bought both—the berries for Jaquis, out of which he built strange pies, and the moccasins for himself. He called them his night slippers, but as a matter of fact there was no night on the Athabasca at that time. The day was divided into three shifts, one long and two short ones,—daylight, dusk, and dawn. So it was daylight when the Belle first fixed her large dark eyes upon the strong, handsome face of Smith the Silent, as he sat on his camp stool, bent above a map he was making. Belle's mother, being old in years and unafraid, came close, looked at the picture for a moment, and exclaimed: "Him Jasper Lake," pointing up the Athabasca.

"You know Jasper Lake?" asked the engineer, glancing up for the first time.

"Oui," said the old woman (Belle's step-father was half French); "know 'im ver' well."

Smith looked her over as a matter of habit, for he allowed no man or woman to get by him with the least bit of information concerning the country through which his imaginary line lay. Then he glanced at Belle for fully five seconds, then back to his blue print. Nobody but a he-nun, or a man already wedded to the woods, could do that, but to the credit of the camp it will go down that the chief was the only man in the outfit who failed to feel her presence. As for Jaquis, the alloyed Siwash, he carried the scar of that first meeting for six months, and may, for aught I know, take it with him to his little swinging grave. Even Smith remembers to this day how she looked, standing there on her two trim ankles, that disappeared into her hand-turned sandals or faded in the flute and fringe of her fawn skin skirt. Her full bosom rose and fell, and you could count the beat of her wild heart in the throb of her throat. Her cheeks showed a faint flush of red through the dark olive,—the flush of health and youth,—her nostrils dilated, like those of an Ontario high-jumper, as she drank life from the dewy morn, while her eye danced with the joy of being alive. Jaquis sized and summed her up in the one word "magnific." But in that moment, when she caught the keen, piercing eye of the engineer, the Belle had a stroke that comes sooner or later to all these wild creatures of the wilderness, but comes to most people but once in a lifetime. She never forgot the gleam of that one glance, though the Silent one was innocent enough.

It was during the days that followed, when she sat and watched him at his work, or followed him for hours in the mountain fastnesses, that the Belle of Athabasca lost her heart.

When he came upon a bit of wild scenery and stopped to photograph it, the Belle stood back of him, watching his every movement, and when he passed on she followed, keeping always out of sight.

The Belle's mother haunted him. As often as he broke camp and climbed a little higher upstream, the brown mother moved also, and with her the Belle.

"What does this old woman want?" asked the engineer of Jaquis one evening when, returning to his tent, he found the fat Cree and her daughter camping on his trail.

"She want that pot," said Jaquis.

"Then for the love of We-sec-e-gea, god of the Crees," said Smith, "give it into her hands and bid her begone."

Jaquis did as directed, and the old Indian went away, but she left the girl.

The next day Smith started on a reconnoissance that would occupy three or four days. As he never knew himself when he would return, he never took the trouble to inform Jaquis, the tail of the family.

After breakfast the Belle went over to her mother's. She would have lunched with her mother from the much coveted kettle, but the Belle's mother told her that she should return to the camp of the white man, who was now her lord and master. So the Belle went back and lunched with Jaquis, who otherwise must have lunched alone. Jaquis tried to keep her, and wooed her in his half-wild way; but to her sensitive soul he was repulsive. Moreover, she felt that in some mysterious manner her mother had transferred her, together with her love and allegiance, to Smith the Silent, and to him she must be true. Therefore she returned to the Cree camp.

As the sinking sun neared the crest of the Rockies, the young Indian walked back to the engineer's camp. As she strode along the new trail she plucked wildflowers by the wayside and gathered leaves and wove them into vari-colored wreaths, swinging along with the easy grace of a wild deer.

Now some women would say she had not much to make her happy, but she was happy nevertheless. She loved a man—to her the noblest, most god-like creature of his kind,—and she was happy in abandoning herself to him. She had lived in this love so long, had felt and seen it grow from nothing to something formidable, then to something fine, until now it filled her and thrilled her; it overspread everything, outran her thoughts, brought the far-off mountains nearer, shortened the trail between her camp and his, gave a new glow to the sunset, a new glory to the dawn and a fresher fragrance to the wildflowers; the leaves whispered to her, the birds came, nearer and sang sweeter; in short it was her life—the sunshine of her soul. And that's the way a wild woman loves.

And she was to see him soon. Perhaps he would speak to her, or smile on her. If only he gave a passing glance she would be glad and content to know that he was near. Alas, he came not at all. She watched with the stars through the short night, slept at dawn, and woke to find Jaquis preparing the morning meal. She thought to question Jaquis, but her interest in the engineer, and the growing conviction that his own star sank as his master's rose, rendered him unsafe as a companion to a young bride whose husband was in the hills and unconscious of the fact that he was wedded to anything save the wilderness and his work.

Jaquis not only refused to tell her where the engineer was operating, but promised to strangle her if she mentioned his master's name again.

At last the long day died, the sunset was less golden, and the stars sang sadder than they sang the day before. She watched the west, into which he had gone and out of which she hoped he might return to her. Another round of dusk and dawn and there came another day, with its hours that hung like ages. When she sighed her mother scolded and Jaquis swore. When at last night came to curtain the hills, she stole out under the stars and walked and walked until the next day dawned. A lone wolf howled to his kith, but they were not hungry and refused to answer his call. Often, in the dark, she fancied she heard faint, feline footsteps behind her. Once a big black bear blocked her trail, staring at her with lifted muzzle wet with dew and stained with berry juice. She did not faint nor scream nor stay her steps, but strode on. Now nearer and nearer came the muffled footsteps behind her. The black bear backed from the trail and kept backing, pivoting slowly, like a locomotive on a turntable, and as she passed on, stood staring after her, his small eyes blinking in babylike bewilderment. And so through the dusk and dark and dawn this love-mad maiden walked the wilderness, innocent of arms, and with no one near to protect her save the little barefooted bowman whom the white man calls the God of Love.

Meanwhile away to the west, high in the hills, where the Findlay flowing into the Pine makes the Peace, then cutting through the crest of the continent makes a path for the Peace, Smith and his little army, isolated, remote, with no cable connecting them with the great cities of civilization, out of touch with the telegraph, away from the war correspondent, with only the music of God's rills for a regimental band, were battling bravely in a war that can end only with the conquest of a wilderness. Ah, these be the great generals—these unheralded heroes who, while the smoke of slaughter smudges the skies and shadows the sun, wage a war in which they kill only time and space, and in the end, without despoiling the rest of the world, win homes for the homeless. These are the heroes of the Anglo-Saxon race.

Finding no trace of the trail-makers, the Belle faced the rising sun and sought the camp of the Crees.

The mysterious shadow with the muffled tread, that had followed her from the engineer's camp, shrank back into the bush as she passed down the trail. That was Jaquis. He watched her as she strode by him, uncertain as to whether he loved or hated her, for well he knew why she walked the wilderness all night alone. Now the Gitche in his unhappy heart made him long to lift her in his arms and carry her to camp, and then the bad god, Mitche, would assert himself and say to the savage that was in him, "Go, kill her. She despises her race and flings herself at the white man's feet." And so, impelled by passion and stayed by love, he followed her. The white man within him made him ashamed of his skulking, and the Indian that was in him guided him around her and home by a shorter trail.

That night the engineers returned, and when Smith saw the Cree in the camp he jumped on Jaquis furiously.

"Why do you keep this woman here?" he demanded.

"I—keep? Me?" quoth Jaquis, blinking as bewildered as the black bear had blinked at the Belle.

"Who but you?—you heathen!" hissed the engineer.

Now Jaquis, calling up the ghosts of his dead sires, asserted that it was the engineer himself who was "keeping" the Cree. "You bought her—she's yours," said Jaquis, in the presence of the company.

"You ill-bred ——" Smith choked, and reached for a tent prop. The next moment his hand was at the Indian's throat. With a quick twist of his collar band he shut off the Siwash's wind, choking him to the earth.

"What do you mean?" he demanded, and Jaquis, coughing, put up his hands. "I meant no lie," said he. "Did you not give to her mother the camp kettle? She has it, marked G.T.P."

"And what of that?"

"Voilà," said Jaquis, "because of that she gave to you the Belle of Athabasca."

Smith dropped his stick, releasing the Indian.

"I did not mean she is sold to you. She is trade—trade for the empty pot, the Belle—the beautiful. From yesterday to this day she followed you, far, very far, to the foot of the Grande Côte, and nothing harmed her. The mountain lion looked on her in terror, the timber wolf took to the hills, the black bear backed from the trail and let her pass in peace," said Jaquis, with glowing enthusiasm. It was the first time he had talked of her, save to the stars and to We-sec-e-gea, and he glowed and grew eloquent in praise of her.

"You take her," said Smith, with one finger levelled at the head of the cook, "to the camp of the Crees. Say to her mother that your master is much obliged for the beautiful gift, but he's too busy to get married and too poor to support a wife."

From the uttermost rim of the ring of light that came from the flickering fire la Belle the beautiful heard and saw all that had passed between the two men. She did not throw herself at the feet of the white man. Being a wild woman she did not weep nor cry out with the pain of his words, that cut like cold steel into her heart. She leaned against an aspen tree, stroking her throat with her left hand, swallowing with difficulty. Slowly from her girdle she drew a tiny hunting-knife, her one weapon, and toyed with it. She put the hilt to the tree, the point to her bare breast, and breathed a prayer to We-sec-e-gea, god of the Crees. She had only to throw the weight of her beautiful body on the blade, sink without a moan to the moss, and pass, leaving the camp undisturbed.

Smith marked the faintest hint of sarcasm in the half smile of the Indian as he turned away.

"Come here," he cried. Jaquis approached cautiously. "Now, you skulking son of a Siwash, this is to be skin for skin. If any harm comes to that young Cree you go to your little hammock in the hemlocks—you understand?"

"Oui, Monsieur," said Jaquis.

"Very well, then; remember—skin for skin."

Now to the Belle, watching from her shelter in the darkness, there was something splendid in this. To hear her praises sung by the Siwash, then to have the fair god, who had heard that story, champion her, to take the place of her protector, was all new to her. "Ah, good God," she sighed; "it is better, a thousand times better, to love and lose him than to waste one's life, never knowing this sweet agony."

She felt in a vague way that she was soaring above the world and its woes. At times, in the wild tumult of her tempestuous soul, she seemed to be borne beyond it all, through beautiful worlds. Love, for her, had taken on great white wings, and as he wafted her out of the wilderness and into her heaven, his talons tore into her heart and hurt like hell, yet she could rejoice because of the exquisite pleasure that surpassed the pain.

"Sweet We-sec-e-gea," she sighed, "good god of my dead, I thank thee for the gift of this great love that stays the steel when my aching heart yearns for it. I shall not destroy myself and distress him, disturbing him in his great work, whatever it is; but live—live and love him, even though he send me away."

She kissed the burnished blade and returned it to her belt.

When Jaquis, circling the camp, failed to find her, he guessed that she was gone, and hurried after her along the dim, starlit trail. When he had overtaken her, they walked on together. Jaquis tried now to renew his acquaintance with the handsome Cree and to make love to her. She heard him in absolute silence. Finally, as they were nearing the Cree camp, he taunted her with having been rejected by the white man.

"And my shame is yours," said she softly. "I love him; he sends me away. You love me; I send you from me—it is the same."

Jaquis, quieted by this simple statement, said good-night and returned to the tents, where the pathfinders were sleeping peacefully under the stars.

And over in the Cree camp the Belle of Athabasca, upon her bed of boughs, slept the sleep of the innocent, dreaming sweet dreams of her fair god, and through them ran a low, weird song of love, and in her dream Love came down like a beautiful bird and bore her out of this life and its littleness, and though his talons tore at her heart and hurt, yet was she happy because of the exquisite pleasure that surpassed all pain.

PATHFINDING IN THE NORTHWEST

It was summer when my friend Smith, whose real name is Jones, heard that the new transcontinental line would build by the way of Peace River Pass to the Pacific. He immediately applied, counting something, no doubt, on his ten years of field work in Washington, Oregon, and other western states, and five years pathfinding in Canada.

The summer died; the hills and rills and the rivers slept, but while they slept word came to my friend Smith the Silent, and he hurriedly packed his sleds and set out.

His orders were, like the orders of Admiral Dewey, to do certain things—not merely to try. He was to go out into the northern night called winter, feel his way up the Athabasca, over the Smoky, follow the Peace River, and find the pass through the Rockies.

If the simple story of that winter campaign could be written out it would be finer than fiction. But it will never be. Only Smith the Silent knows, and he won't tell.

Sometimes, over the pipe, he forgets and gives me glimpses into the winter camp, with the sun going out like a candle: the hastily made camp with the half-breed spotting the dry wood against the coming moment when night would drop over the forest like a curtain over a stage; the "lean-to" between the burning logs, where he dozes or dreams, barely beyond the reach of the flames; the silence all about, Jaquis pulling at his pipe, and the huskies sleeping in the snow like German babies under the eiderdown. Sometimes, out of the love of bygone days, he tells of long toilsome journeys with the sun hiding behind clouds out of which an avalanche of snow falls, with nothing but the needle to tell where he hides; of hungry dogs and half starved horses, and lakes and rivers fifty and a hundred miles out of the way.

Once, he told me, he sent an engineer over a low range to spy out a pass. By the maps and other data they figured that he would be gone three days, but a week went by and no word from the pathfinder. Ten days and no news. On the thirteenth day, when Smith was preparing to go in search of the wanderer, the running gear of the man and the framework of the dogs came into camp. He was able to smile and say to Smith that he had been ten days without food, save a little tea. For the dogs he had had nothing.

A few days rest and they were on the trail again, or on the "go" rather; and you might know that disciple of Smith the Silent six months or six years before he would, unless you worked him, refer to that ten days' fast. They think no more of that than a Jap does of dying. It's all in the day's work.

Suddenly, Smith said, the sun swung north, the days grew longer. The sun grew hot and the snow melted on the south hills; the hushed rivers, rending their icy bonds, went roaring down to the Lakes and out towards the Arctic Ocean. And lo, suddenly, like the falling of an Arctic night, the momentary spring passed and it was summer time.

Then it was that Smith came into Edmonton to make his first report, and here we met for the first time for many snows.

Joyously, as a boy kicks the cover off on circus morning, this Northland flings aside her winter wraps and stands forth in her glorious garb of summer. The brooklets murmur, the rivers sing, and by their banks and along the lakes waterfowl frolic, and overhead glad birds, that seem to have dropped from the sky, sing joyfully the almost endless song of summer. At the end of the long day, when the sun, as if to make up for its absence, lingers, loath to leave us in the twilight, beneath their wings the song-birds hide their heads, then wake and sing, for the sun is swinging up over the horizon where the pink sky, for an hour, has shown the narrow door through which the day is dawning.

The dogs and sleds have been left behind and now, with Jaquis the half-breed "boy" leading, followed closely by Smith the Silent, we go deeper and deeper each day into the pathless wilderness.

To be sure it is not all bush, all forest. At times we cross wide reaches of wild prairie lands. Sometimes great lakes lie immediately in front of us, compelling us to change our course. Now we come to a wide river and raft our outfit over, swimming our horses. Weeks go by and we begin to get glimpses of the Rockies rising above the forest, and we push on. The streams become narrower as we ascend, but swifter and more dangerous.

We do not travel constantly now, as we have been doing. Sometimes we keep our camp for two or three days. The climbing is hard, for Smith must get to the top of every peak in sight, and so I find it "good hunting" about the camp.

Jaquis is a fairly good cook, and what he lacks we make up with good appetites, for we live almost constantly out under the sun and stars.

Pathfinders always lay up on Sunday, and sometimes, the day being long, Smith steals out to the river and comes back with a mountain trout as long as a yardstick.

The scenery is beyond description. Now we pass over the shoulder of a mountain with a river a thousand feet below. Sometimes we trail for hours along the shore of a limpid lake that seems to run away to the foot of the Rockies.

Far away we get glimpses of the crest of the continent, where the Peace River gashes it as if it had been cleft by the sword of the Almighty; and near the Rockies, on either bank, grand battlements rise that seem to guard the pass as the Sultan's fortresses frown down on the Dardanelles.

Now we follow a narrow trail that was not a trail until we passed. A careless pack-horse, carrying our blankets, slips from the path and goes rolling and tumbling down the mountain side. A thousand feet below lies an arm of the Athabasca. Down, down, and over and over the pack-horse goes, and finally fetches up on a ledge five hundred feet below the trail. "By damn," says Jaquis, "dere is won bronco bust, eh?"

Smith and Jaquis go down to cut the cinches and save the pack, and lo, up jumps our cayuse, and when he is repacked he takes the trail as good as new. The pack and the low bush save his life.

In any other country, to other men, this would be exciting, but it's all in the day's work with Smith and Jaquis.

The pack-pony that had been down the mountain is put in the lead now—that is, in the lead of the pack animals; for he has learned his lesson, he will be careful. And yet we are to have other experiences along this same river.

Suddenly, down a side cañon, a mountain stream rushes, plunging into the Athabasca, joyfully, like a sea-bather into the surf. Jaquis calls this side-stream "the mill-tail o' hell." Smith the Silent prepares to cross. It's all very simple. All you need is a stout pole, a steady nerve, and an utter disregard for the hereafter.

When Smith is safe on the other shore we drive the horses into the stream. They shudder and shrink from the ice-cold water, but Jaquis and I urge them, and in they plunge. My, what a struggle! Their wet feet on the slippery boulders in the bottom of the stream, the swift current constantly tripping them—it was thrilling to see and must have been agony for the animals.

Midway, where the current was strongest, a mouse-colored cayuse carrying a tent lost his feet. The turbulent tide slammed him up on top of a great rock, barely hidden beneath the water, and he got to his feet like a cat that has fallen upon the edge of an eave-trough. Trembling, the cayuse called to Smith, and Smith, running downstream, called back, urging the animal to leave the refuge and swim for it. The pack-horse perched on the rock gazes wistfully at the shore. The waters, breaking against his resting-place, wash up to his trembling knees. About him the wild river roars, and just below leaps over a ten-foot fall into the Athabasca.

All the other horses, having crossed safely, shake the water from their dripping sides and begin cropping the tender grass. We could have heard that horse's heart beat if we could have hushed the river's roar.

Smith called again, the cayuse turned slightly, and whether he leaped deliberately or his feet slipped on the slippery stones, forcing him to leap, we could not say, but he plunged suddenly into the stream, uttering a cry that echoed up the cañon and over the river like the cry of a lost soul.

The cruel current caught him, lifted him, and plunged him over the drop, and he was lost instantly in the froth and foam of the falls.

Far down, at a bend of the Athabasca, something white could be seen drifting towards the shore. That night Smith the Silent made an entry in his little red book marked "Grand Trunk Pacific," and tented under the stars.

THE CURÉ'S CHRISTMAS GIFT

"A country that is bad or good,
Precisely as your claim pans out;
A land that's much misunderstood,
Misjudged, maligned and lied about."

When the pathfinders for the New National Highway pushed open the side door and peeped through to the Pacific they not only discovered a short cut to Yokohama, but opened to the world a new country, revealing the last remnant of the Last West.

Edmonton is the outfiting point, of course, but Little Slave Lake is the real gateway to the wilderness. Here we were to make our first stop (we were merely exploring), and from this point our first portage was to the Peace River, at Chinook, where we would get into touch once more with the Hudson's Bay Company.

Jim Cromwell, the free trader who was in command of Little Slave, made us welcome, introducing us ensemble to his friend, a former H.B. factor, to the Yankee who was looking for a timber limit, to the "Literary Cuss," as he called the young man in corduroys and a wide white hat, who was endeavoring to get past "tradition," that has damned this Dominion both in fiction and in fact for two hundred years, and do something that had in it the real color of the country.

At this point the free trader paused to assemble the Missourian. This iron-gray individual shook himself out, came forward, and gripped our hands, one after another.

The free trader would not allow us to make camp that night. We were sentenced to sup and lodge with him, furnishing our own bedding, of course, but baking his bread.

The smell of cooking coffee and the odor of frying fish came to us from the kitchen, and floating over from somewhere the low, musical, well modulated voice of Cromwell, conversing in Cree, as he moved about among his mute and apparently inoffensive camp servants.

The day died hard. The sun was still shining at 9 p.m. At ten it was twilight, and in the dusk we sat listening to tales of the far North, totally unlike the tales we read in the story-books. Smith the Silent, who was in charge of our party, was interested in the country, of course, its physical condition, its timber, its coal, and its mineral possibilities. He asked about its mountains and streams, its possible and impossible passes; but the "Literary Cuss" and I were drinking deeply of weird stories that were being told quite incautiously by the free trader, the old factor, and by the Missourian. We were like children, this young author and I, sitting for the first time in a theatre. The flickering camp fire that we had kindled in the open served as a footlight, while the Gitch Lamp, still gleaming in the west, glanced through the trees and lit up the faces of the three great actors who were entertaining us without money and without price. The Missourian was the star. He had been reared in the lap of luxury, had run away from college where he had been installed by a rich uncle, his guardian, and jumped down to South America. He had ridden with the Texas Rangers and with President Diaz's Regulators, had served as a scout on the plains and worked with the Mounted Police, but was now "retired."

All of which we learned not from him directly, but from the stories he told and from his bosom friend, the free trader, whose guests we were, and whose word, for the moment at least, we respected.

The camp fire burned down to a bed of coals, the Gitch Lamp went out. In the west, now, there was only a glow of gold, but no man moved.

Smith the Pathfinder and our host the free trader bent over a map. "But isn't this map correct?" Smith would ask, and when in doubt Jim would call the Missourian. "No," said the latter, "you can't float down that river because it flows the other way, and that range of mountains is two hundred miles out."

Gradually we became aware that all this vast wilderness, to the world unknown, was an open book to this quiet man who had followed the buffalo from the Rio Grande to the Athabasca where he turned, made a last stand, and then went down.

When the rest had retired the free trader and I sat talking of the Last West, of the new trail my friends were blazing, and of the wonderfully interesting individual whom we called the Missourian.

"He had a prospecting pard," said Jim, "whom he idolized. This man, whose name was Ramsey, Jack Ramsey, went out in '97 between the Coast Range and the Rockies, and now this sentimental old pioneer says he will never leave the Peace River until he finds Ramsey's bones.

"You see," Cromwell continued, "friendship here and what goes for friendship outside are vastly different. The matter of devoting one's life to a friend or to a duty, real or fancied, is only a trifle to these men who abide in the wilderness. I know of a Chinaman and a Cree who lived and died the most devoted friends. You see the Missourian hovering about the last camping-place of his companion. Behold the factor! He has left the Hudson Bay Company after thirty years because he has lost his life's best friend, a man who spoke another language, whose religion was not the brand upon which the factor had been brought up in England; yet they were friends."

The camp fire had gone out. In the south we saw the first faint flush of dawn as Cromwell, knocking the ashes from his pipe, advised me to go to bed. "You get the old factor to tell you the story of his friend the curé, and of the curé's Christmas gift," Cromwell called back, and I made a point of getting the story, bit by bit, from the florid factor himself, and you shall read it as it has lingered in my memory.

When the new curé came to Chinook on the Upper Peace River, he carried a small hand-satchel, his blankets, and a crucifix. His face was drawn, his eyes hungry, his frame wasted, but his smile was the smile of a man at peace with the world. The West—the vast, undiscovered Canadian West—jarred on the sensitive nerves of this Paris-bred priest. And yet, when he crossed the line that marks what we are pleased to call "civilization," and had reached the heart of the real Northwest, where the people were unspoiled, natural, and honest, where a handful of Royal Northwest Mounted Police kept order in an empire that covers a quarter of a continent, he became deeply interested in this new world, in the people, in the imperial prairies, the mountains, and the great wide rivers that were racing down to the northern sea.

The factor at the Hudson's Bay post, whose whole life since he had left college in England had been passed on the Peace River, at York Factory, and other far northern stations over which waved the Hudson's Bay banner, warmed to the new curé from their first meeting, and the curé warmed to him. Each seemed to find in the other a companion that neither had been able to find among the few friends of his own faith.

And so, through the long evenings of the northern winter, they sat in the curé's cabin study or by the factor's fire, and talked of the things which they found interesting, including politics, literature, art, and Indians. Despite the great gulf that rolled between the two creeds in which they had been cradled, they found that they were in accord three times in five—a fair average for men of strong minds and inherent prejudices. At first the curé was anxious to get at the real work of "civilizing" the natives.

"Yes," the factor would say, blowing the smoke upward, "the Indian should be civilized—slowly—the slower the better."

The curé would pretend to look surprised as he relit his pipe. Once the curé asked the factor why he was so indifferent to the welfare of the Crees, who were the real producers, without whose furs there would be no trade, no post, no job for the ruddy-faced factor. The priest was surprised that the factor should appear to fail to appreciate the importance of the trapper.

"I do," said the factor.

"Then why do you not help us to lift him to the light?"

"I like him," was the laconic reply.

"Then why don't you talk to him of his soul?"

"Haven't the nerve," said the factor, shaking his head and blowing more smoke.

The curé shrugged his shoulders.

"I say," said the florid factor, facing the pale priest. "Did you see me decorating the old chief, Dunraven, yesterday?"

"Yes, I presume you were giving him a pour boire in advance to secure the greater catch of furs next season," said the priest, with his usual sad yet always pleasant smile.

"A very poor guess for one so wise," said the factor. "Attendez," he continued. "This post used to be closed always in winter. The tent doors were tied fast on the inside, after which the man who tied them would crawl out under the edge of the canvas. When winter came, the snow, banked about, held the tent tightly down, and the Hudson's Bay business was bottled at this point until the springless summer came to wake the sleeping world.

"Last winter was a hard winter. The snow was deep and game scarce. One day a Cree Indian found himself in need of tea and tobacco, and more in need of a new pair of trousers. Passing the main tent one day, he was sorely tempted. Dimly, through the parchment pane, he could see great stacks of English tweeds, piles of tobacco, and boxes of tea, but the tent was closed. He was sorely tried. He was hungry—hungry for a horn of tea and a twist of the weed, and cold, too. Ah, bon père, it is hard to withstand cold and hunger with only a canvas between one and the comforts of life!"

"Oui, Monsieur!" said the curé, warmly, touched by the pathos of the tale.

"The Indian walked away (we know that by his footprints), but returned to the tent. The hunger and the cold had conquered. He took his hunting-knife and slit the deerskin window and stepped inside. Then he approached the pile of tweed trousers and selected a large pair, putting down from the bunch of furs he had on his arms to the value of eight skins—the price his father and grandfather had paid. He visited the tobacco pile and helped himself, leaving four skins on the tobacco. When he had taken tea he had all his heart desired, and having still a number of skins left, he hung them upon a hook overhead and went away.

"When summer dawned and a clerk came to open the post, he saw the slit in the window, and upon entering the tent saw the eight skins on the stack of tweeds, the four skins on the tobacco, and the others on the chest, and understood.

"Presently he saw the skins which the Indian had hung upon the hook, took them down, counted them carefully, appraised them, and made an entry in the Receiving Book, in which he credited 'Indian-cut-the-window, 37 skins.'

"Yesterday Dunraven came to the post and confessed.

"It was to reward him for his honesty that I gave him the fur coat and looped the big brass baggage check in his buttonhole. Voilà!"

The curé crossed his legs and then recrossed them, tossed his head from side to side, drummed upon the closed book which lay in his lap, and showed in any number of ways, peculiar to nervous people, his amazement at the story and his admiration for the Indian.

"Little things like that," said the factor, filling his pipe, "make me timid when talking to a Cree about 'being good.'"

When summer came, and with it the smell of flowers and the music of running streams, the factor and his friend the curé used to take long tramps up into the highlands, but the curé's state of health was a handicap to him. The factor saw the telltale flush in the priest's face and knew that the "White Plague" had marked him; yet he never allowed the curé to know that he knew. That summer a little river steamer was sent up from Athabasca Lake by the Chief Commissioner who sat in the big office at Winnipeg, and upon this the factor and his friend took many an excursion up and down the Peace. The friendship that had grown up between the factor and the new curé formed the one slender bridge that connected the Anglican and the Catholic camps. Even the "heathen Crees" marvelled that these white men, praying to the same God, should dwell so far apart. Wing You, who had wandered over from Ramsay's Camp on the Pine River, explained it all to Dunraven: "Flenchman and Englishman," said Wing. "No ketchem same Glod. You—Clee," continued the wise Oriental, "an' Englishman good flend—ketchem same Josh; you call 'im We-sec-e-gea, white man call 'im God."

And so, having the same God, only called by different names, the Crees trusted the factor, and the factor trusted the Crees. Their business intercourse was on the basis of skin for skin, furs being the recognized coin of the country.

"Why do you not pay them in cash, take cash in turn, and let them have something to rattle?" asked the curé one day.

"They won't have it," said the factor. "Silver Skin, brother to Dunraven, followed a party of prospectors out to Edmonton last fall and tried it. He bought a pair of gloves, a red handkerchief, and a pound of tobacco, and emptied his pockets on the counter, so that the clerk in the shop might take out the price of the goods. According to his own statement, the Indian put down $37.80. He took up just six-thirty-five. When the Cree came back to God's country he showed me what he had left and asked me to check him up. When I had told him the truth, he walked to the edge of the river and sowed the six-thirty-five broadcast on the broad bosom of the Peace."

And so, little by little, the patient priest got the factor's view-point, and learned the great secret of the centuries of success that has attended the Hudson's Bay Company in the far North.

And little by little the two men, without preaching, revealed to the Indians and the Oriental the mystery of Life—vegetable life at first—of death and life beyond. They showed them the miracle of the wheat.

On the first day of June they put into a tiny grave a grain of wheat. They told the Blind Ones that the berry would suffer death, decay, but out of that grave would spring fresh new flags that would grow and blow, tanned by the balmy chinook winds, and wet by the dews of heaven.

On the first day of September they harvested seventy-two stalks and threshed from the seventy-two stalks seven thousand two hundred grains of wheat. They showed all this to the Blind Ones and they saw. The curé explained that we, too, would go down and die, but live again in another life, in a fairer world.

The Cree accepted it all in absolute silence, but the Oriental, with his large imagination, exclaimed, pointing to the tiny heap of golden grain: "Me ketchem die, me sleep, byme by me wake up in China—seven thousand—heap good." The curé was about to explain when the factor put up a warning finger. "Don't cut it too fine, father," said he. "They're getting on very well."

That was a happy summer for the two men, working together in the garden in the cool dawn and chatting in the long twilight that lingers on the Peace until 11 p.m. Alas! as the summer waned the factor saw that his friend was failing fast. He could walk but a short distance now without resting, and when the red rose of the Upper Athabasca caught the first cold kiss of Jack Frost, the good priest took to his bed. Wing You, the accomplished cook, did all he could to tempt him to eat and grow strong again. Dunraven watched from day to day for an opportunity to "do something"; but in vain. The faithful factor made daily visits to the bedside of his sick friend. As the priest, who was still in the springtime of his life, drew nearer to the door of death, he talked constantly of his beloved mother in far-off France—a thing unusual for a priest, who is supposed to burn his bridges when he leaves the world for the church.

Often when he talked thus, the factor wanted to ask his mother's name and learn where she lived, but always refrained.

Late in the autumn the factor was called to Edmonton for a general conference of all the factors in the employ of the Honorable Company of gentlemen adventurers trading into Hudson's Bay. With a heavy heart he said good-bye to the failing priest.

When he had come within fifty miles of Chinook, on the return trip, he was wakened at midnight by Dunraven, who had come out to ask him to hurry up as the curé was dying, but wanted to speak to the factor first.

Without a word the Englishman got up and started forward, Dunraven leading on the second lap of his "century."

It was past midnight again when the voyageurs arrived at the river. There was a dim light in the curé's cabin, to which Dunraven led them, and where the Catholic bishop and an Irish priest were on watch. "So glad to see you," said the bishop. "There is something he wants from your place, but he will not tell Wing. Speak to him, please."

"Ah, Monsieur, I'm glad that you are come—I'm weary and want to be off."

"The long traverse, eh?"

"Oui, Monsieur—le grand voyage."

"Is there anything I can do for you?" asked the Englishman. The dying priest made a movement as if hunting for something. The bishop, to assist, stepped quickly to his side. The patient gave up the quest of whatever he was after and looked languidly at the factor. "What is it, my son?" asked the bishop, bending low. "What would you have the factor fetch from his house?"

"Just a small bit of cheese," said the sick man, sighing wearily.

"Now, that's odd," mused the factor, as he went off on his strange errand.

When the Englishman returned to the cabin, the bishop and the priest stepped outside for a breath of fresh air. Upon a bench on the narrow veranda Dunraven sat, resting after his hundred-mile tramp, and on the opposite side of the threshold Wing You lay sleeping in his blankets, so as to be in easy call if he were wanted.

When the two friends were alone, the sick man signalled, and the factor drew near.

"I have a great favor—a very great favor to ask of you," the priest began, "and then I'm off. Ah, mon Dieu!" he panted. "It has been hard to hold out. Jesus has been kind."

"It's damned tough at your time, old fellow," said the factor, huskily.

"It's not my time, but His."

"Yes—well I shall be over by and by."

"And those faithful dogs—Dunraven and Wing—thank them for—"

"Sure! If I can pass," the factor broke in, a little confused.

"Thank them for me—for their kindnesses—and care. Tell them to remember the sermon of the wheat. And now, good friend," said the priest, summoning all his strength, "attendez!"

He drew a thin, white hand from beneath the cover, carrying a tiny crucifix. "I want you to send this to my beloved mother by registered post; send it yourself, please, so that she may have it before the end of the year. This will be my last Christmas gift to her. And the one that comes from her to me—that is for you, to keep in remembrance of me. And write to her—oh, so gently tell her—Jesus—help me," he gasped, sitting upright. "She lives in Rue ——— O Mary, Mother of Jesus," he cried, clutching at the collar of his gown; and then he fell back upon his bed, and his soul swept skyward like a toy balloon when the thin thread snaps.

When the autumn sun smiled down on Chinook and the autumn wind sighed in by the door and out by the open window where the dead priest lay, Wing and Dunraven sat on the rude bench in the little veranda, going over it all, each in his own tongue, but uttering never a word, yet each to the other expressing the silence of his soul.

The factor, in the seclusion of his bachelor home, held the little cross up and examined it critically. "To be sent to his mother, she lives in Rue ——— Ah, if I could have been but a day sooner; yet the bishop must know," he added, putting the crucifix carefully away.

The good people in the other world, beyond the high wall that separated the two Christian Tribes, had been having shivers over the factor and his fondness for the Romans; but when he volunteered to assist at the funeral of his dead friend, his people were shocked. In that scant settlement there were not nearly enough priests to perform, properly, the funeral services, so the factor fell in, mingling his deep full voice with the voices of the bishop and the Irish brother, and grieving even as they grieved.

And the Blind Ones, Wing and Dunraven, came also, paying a last tearless tribute to the noble dead.

When it was all over and the post had settled down to routine, the factor found in his mail, one morning, a long letter from the Chief Commissioner at Winnipeg. It told the factor that he was in bad repute, that the English Church bishop had been grieved, shocked, and scandalized through seeing the hitherto respectable factor going over to the Catholics. Not only had he fraternized with them, but had actually taken part in their religious ceremonies. And to crown it all, he had carried, a respectable Cree and the Chinese cook along with him.

The factor's placid face took on a deep hue, but only for a moment. He filled his pipe, poking the tobacco down hard with his thumb. Then he took the Commissioner's letter, twisted it up, touched it to the tiny fire that blazed in the grate, and lighted his pipe. He smoked in silence for a few moments and then said to himself, being alone, "Huh!"

"Ah, that from the bishop reminds me," said the factor. "I must run over and see the other one."

When the factor had related to the French-Canadian bishop what had passed between the dead curé and himself, the bishop seemed greatly annoyed. "Why, man, he had no mother!"

"The devil he didn't—I beg pardon—I say he asked me to send this to his mother. He started to tell me where she lived and then the call came. It was the dying request of a dear friend. I beg of you tell me his mother's name, that I may keep my word."

"It is impossible, my son. When he came into the church he left the world. He was bound by the law of the church to give up father, mother, sister, brother—all."

"The church be—do you mean to say—"

"Peace, my son, you do not understand," said the bishop, lifting the little cross which he had taken gently from the factor at the beginning of the interview.

Now the factor was not in the habit of having his requests ignored and his judgment questioned.

"Do you mean to say you will not give me the name and address of the dead man's mother?"

"It's absolutely impossible. Moreover, I am shocked to learn that our late brother could so far forget his duty at the very door of death. No, son, a thousand times no," said the bishop.

"Then give me the crucifix!" demanded the factor, fiercely.

"That, too, is impossible; that is the property of the church."

"Well," said the factor, filling his pipe again and gazing into the flickering fire, "they're all about the same. And they're all right, too, I presume—all but Wing and Dunraven and me."

THE MYSTERIOUS SIGNAL

As Waterloo lingered in the memory of the conquered Corsican, so Ashtabula was burned into the brain of Bradish. Out of that awful wreck he crawled, widowed and childless. For a long time he did not realize, for his head was hurt in that frightful crash.

By the time he was fit to leave the hospital they had told him, little by little, that all his people had perished.

He made his way to the West, where he had a good home and houses to rent and a hole in the hillside that was just then being changed from a prospect to a mine.

The townspeople, who had heard of the disaster, waited for him to speak of it—but he never did. The neighbors nodded, and he nodded to them and passed on about his business. The old servant came and asked if she should open the house, and he nodded. The man-servant—the woman's husband—came also, and to him Bradish nodded; and at noon he had luncheon alone in the fine new house that had just been completed a year before the catastrophe.

About once a week Bradish would board the midnight express, ride down the line for a few hundred miles, and double back.

When he went away they knew he had gone, and when he came back they knew he had returned and that was as much as his house-keeper, his agent, or the foreman at the mines could tell you.

One would have thought that the haunting memory of Ashtabula would have kept him at home for the rest of his life; but he seemed to travel for the sake of the ride only, or for no reason, as a deaf man walks on the railroad-track.

Gradually he extended his trips, taking the Midland over into Utah; and once or twice he had been seen on the rear end of the California Limited as it dropped down the western water-shed of Raton Range.

One night, when the Limited was lapping up the landscape and the Desert was rushing in under her pilot and streaking out below the last sleeper like tape from a ticker, the danger signal sounded in the engine cab, the air went on full, the passengers braced themselves against the seats in front of them, or held their breath in their berths as the train came to a dead stop.

The conductor and the head man hurried forward shouting, "What's the matter?" to the engineer.

The driver, leaning from his lofty window, asked angrily, "What in thunder's the matter with you? I got a stop signal from behind."

"You'd better lay off and have a good sleep," said the conductor.

"I'll put you to sleep for a minute if you ever hint that I was not awake coming down Cañon Diablo," shouted the engineer, releasing his brakes. As the long, heavy train glided by, the trainmen swung up like sailors, and away went the Limited over the long bridge, five minutes to the bad.

A month later the same thing happened on the East end. The engineer was signalled and stopped on a curve with the point of his pilot on a high bridge.

This time the captain and the engineer were not so brittle of temper. They discussed the matter, calling on the fireman, who had heard nothing, being busy in the coal-tank.

The head brakeman, crossing himself, said it was the "unseen hand" that had been stopping the Limited on the Desert. It might be a warning, he said, and walked briskly out on the bridge looking for dynamite, ghosts, and things.

When he had reached the other end of the bridge, he gave the go-ahead signal and the train pulled out. As they had lost seven minutes, it was necessary for the conductor to report "cause of delay;" and that was the first hint the officials of any of the Western lines had of the "unseen hand."

Presently trainmen, swapping yarns at division stations, heard of the mysterious signal on other roads.

The Columbia Limited, over on the Short Line, was choked with her head over Snake River, at the very edge of Pendleton. When they had pulled in and a fresh crew had taken the train on, the in-coming captain and his daring driver argued over the incident and they each got ten days,—not for the delay, but because they could not see to sign the call-book next morning and were not fit to be seen by other people.

The next train stopped was the International Limited on the Grand Trunk, then the Sunset by the South Coast.

The strange phenomenon became so general that officials lost patience. One road issued an order to the effect that any engineer who heard signals when there were no signals should get thirty days for the first and his time for the second offence.

Within a week from the appearance of the unusual and unusually offensive bulletin, "Baldy" Hooten heard the stop signal as he neared a little Junction town where his line crossed another on an overhead bridge.

When the signal sounded, the fireman glanced over at the driver, who dived through the window up to his hip pockets.

When the engine had crashed over the bridge, the driver pulled himself into the cab again, and once more the signal. The fireman, amazed, stared at the engineer. The latter jerked the throttle wide open; seeing which, the stoker dropped to the deck and began feeding the hungry furnace. Ten minutes later the Limited screamed for a regular stop, ten miles down the line. As the driver dropped to the ground and began touching the pins and links with the back of his bare hand, to see if they were all cool, the head brakeman trotted forward whispering hoarsely, "The ol' man's aboard."

The driver waved him aside with his flaring torch, and up trotted the blue-and-gold conductor with his little silver white-light with a frosted flue. "Why didn't you stop at Pee-Wee Junction?" he hissed.

"Is Pee-Wee a stop station?"

"On signal."

"I didn't see no sign."

"I pulled the bell."

"Go on now, you ghost-dancer," said the engineer.

"You idiot!" gasped the exasperated conductor. "Don't you know the old man's on, that he wanted to stop at Pee-Wee to meet the G.M. this morning, that a whole engineering outfit will be idle there for half a day, and you'll get the guillotine?"

"Whew, you have shore got 'em."

"Isn't your bell working?" asked a big man who had joined the group under the cab window.

"I think so, sir," said the driver, as he recognized the superintendent. "Johnny, try that cab bell," he shouted, and the fire-boy sounded the big brass gong.

"Why didn't you take it at Pee-Wee?" asked the old man, holding his temper beautifully.

The driver lifted his torch and stared almost rudely into the face of the official in front of him. "Why, Mr. Skidum," said he slowly, "I didn't hear no signal."

The superintendent was blocked.

As he turned and followed the conductor into the telegraph office, the driver, gloating in his high tower of a cab, watched him.

"He's an old darling," said he to the fire-boy, "and I'm ready to die for him any day; but I can't stop for him in the face of bulletin 13. Thirty days for the first offence, and then fire," he quoted, as he opened the throttle and steamed away, four minutes late.

The old man drummed on the counter-top in the telegraph office, and then picked up a pad and wrote a wire to his assistant:—

"Cancel general order No. 13."

The night man slipped out in the dawn and called the day man who was the station master, explaining that the old man was at the station and evidently unhappy.

The agent came on unusually early and endeavored to arrange for a light engine to carry the superintendent back to the Junction.

At the end of three hours they had a freight engine that had left its train on a siding thirty miles away and rolled up to rescue the stranded superintendent.

Now, every railway man knows that when one thing goes wrong on a railroad, two more mishaps are sure to follow; so, when the rescuing crew heard over the wire that the train they had left on a siding, having been butted by another train heading in, had started back down grade, spilled over at the lower switch, and blocked the main line, they began to expect something to happen at home.

However, the driver had to go when the old man was in the cab and the G.M. with a whole army of engineers and workmen waiting for him at Pee-Wee; so he rattled over the switches and swung out on the main line like a man who was not afraid.

Two miles up the road the light engine, screaming through a cut, encountered a flock of sheep, wallowed through them, left the track, and slammed the four men on board up against the side of the cut.

Not a bone was broken, though all of them were sore shaken, the engineer being unconscious when picked up.

"Go back and report," said the old man to the conductor. "You look after the engineer," to the fireman.

"Will you flag west, sir?" asked the conductor.

"Yes,—I'll flag into Pee-Wee," said the old man, limping down the line.

To be sure, the superintendent was an intelligent man and not the least bit superstitious; but he couldn't help, as he limped along, connecting these disasters, remotely at least, with general order No. 13.

In time the "unseen signal" came to be talked of by the officials as well as by train and enginemen. It came up finally at the annual convention of General Passenger Agents at Chicago and was discussed by the engineers at Atlanta, but was always ridiculed by the eastern element.

"I helped build the U.P.," said a Buffalo man, "and I want to tell you high-liners you can't drink squirrel-whiskey at timber-line without seein' things nights."

That ended the discussion.

Probably no road in the country suffered from the evil effects of the mysterious signal as did the Inter-Mountain Air Line.

The regular spotters failed to find out, and the management sent to Chicago for a real live detective who would not be predisposed to accept the "mystery" as such, but would do his utmost to find the cause of a phenomenon that was not only interrupting traffic but demoralizing the whole service.

As the express trains were almost invariably stopped at night, the expert travelled at night and slept by day. Months passed with only two or three "signals." These happened to be on the train opposed to the one in which the detective was travelling at that moment. They brought out another man, and on his first trip, taken merely to "learn the road," the train was stopped in broad daylight. This time the stop proved to be a lucky one; for, as the engineer let off the air and slipped round a curve in a cañon, he found a rock as big as a box car resting on the track.

The detective was unable to say who sounded the signal. The train crew were overawed. They would not even discuss the matter.

With a watchman, unknown to the trainmen, on every train, the officials hoped now to solve the mystery in a very short time.

The old engineer, McNally, who had found the rock in the cañon, had boasted in the lodge-room, in the round-house and out, that if ever he got the "ghost-sign," he'd let her go. Of course he was off his guard this time. He had not expected the "spook-stop" in open day. And right glad he was, too, that he stopped that day.

A fortnight later McNally, on the night run, was going down Crooked Creek Cañon watching the fireworks in the heavens. A black cloud hung on a high peak, and where its sable skirts trailed along the range the lightning leaped and flashed in sheets and chains. Above the roar of wheels he could hear the splash, and once in a while he could feel the spray, of new-made cataracts as the water rushed down the mountain side, choking the culverts.

At Crag View there was, at that time, a high wooden trestle stilted up on spliced spruce piles with the bark on.

It used to creak and crack under the engine when it was new. McNally was nearing it now. It lay, however, just below a deep rock cut that had been made in a mountain crag and beyond a sharp curve.

McNally leaned from his cab window, and when the lightning flashed, saw that the cut was clear of rock and released the brakes slightly to allow the long train to slip through the reverse curve at the bridge. Curves cramp a train, and a smooth runner likes to feel them glide smoothly.

As the black locomotive poked her nose through the cut, the engineer leaned out again; but the after-effect of the flash of lightning left the world in inky blackness.

Back in a darkened corner of the drawing-room of the rearmost sleeper the sleuth snored with both eyes and ears open.

Suddenly he saw a man, fully dressed, leap from a lower berth in the last section and make a grab for the bell-rope. The man missed the rope; and before he could leap again the detective landed on the back of his neck, bearing him down. At that moment the conductor came through; and when he saw the detective pull a pair of bracelets from his hip-pocket, he guessed that the man underneath must be wanted, and joined in the scuffle. In a moment the man was handcuffed, for he really offered no resistance. As they released him he rose, and they squashed him into a seat opposite the section from which he had leaped a moment before. The man looked not at his captors, who still held him, but pressed his face against the window. He saw the posts of the snow-shed passing, sprang up, flung the two men from him as a Newfoundland would free himself from a couple of kittens, lifted his manacled hands, leaped toward the ceiling, and bore down on the signal-rope.

The conductor, in the excitement, yelled at the man, bringing the rear brakeman from the smoking-room, followed by the black boy bearing a shoe-brush.

Once more they bore the bad man down, and then the conductor grabbed the rope and signalled the engineer ahead.

Men leaped from their berths, and women showed white faces between the closely drawn curtains.

Once more the conductor pulled the bell, but the train stood still.

One of the passengers picked up the man's hand-grip that had fallen from his berth, and found that the card held in the leather tag read:

"John Bradish."

"Go forward," shouted the conductor to the rear brakeman, "and get 'em out of here,—tell McNally we've got the ghost."

The detective released his hold on his captive, and the man sank limp in the corner seat.

The company's surgeon, who happened to be on the car, came over and examined the prisoner. The man had collapsed completely.

When the doctor had revived the handcuffed passenger and got him to sit up and speak, the porter, wild-eyed, burst in and shouted: "De bridge is gone."

A death-like hush held the occupants of the car.

"De hangin' bridge is sho' gone," repeated the panting porter, "an' de engine, wi' McNally in de cab's crouchin' on de bank, like a black cat on a well-cu'b. De watah's roahin' in de deep gorge, and if she drap she gwine drag—"

The doctor clapped his hand over the frightened darky's mouth, and the detective butted him out to the smoking-room.

The conductor explained that the porter was crazy, and so averted a panic.

The detective came back and faced the doctor. "Take off the irons," said the surgeon, and the detective unlocked the handcuffs.

Now the doctor, in his suave, sympathetic way, began to question Bradish; and Bradish began to unravel the mystery, pausing now and again to rest, for the ordeal through which he had just passed had been a great mental and nervous strain.

He began by relating the Ashtabula accident that had left him wifeless and childless, and, as the story progressed, seemed to find infinite relief in relating the sad tale of his lonely life. It was like a confession. Moreover, he had kept the secret so long locked in his troubled breast that it was good to pour it out.

The doctor sat directly in front of the narrator, the detective beside him, while interested passengers hung over the backs of seats and blocked the narrow aisle. Women, with faces still blanched, sat up in bed listening breathlessly to the strange story of John Bradish.

Shortly after returning to their old home, he related, he was awakened one night by the voice of his wife calling in agonized tones, "John! John!" precisely as she had cried to him through the smoke and steam and twisted débris at Ashtabula. He leaped from his bed, heard a mighty roar, saw a great light flash on his window, and the midnight express crashed by.

To be sure it was only a dream, he said to himself, intensified by the roar of the approaching train; and yet he could sleep no more that night. Try as he would, he could not forget it; and soon he realized that a growing desire to travel was coming upon him. In two or three days' time this desire had become irresistible. He boarded the midnight train and took a ride. But this did not cure him. In fact, the more he travelled the more he wanted to travel. Soon after this he discovered that he had acquired another habit. He wanted to stop the train. Against these inclinations he had struggled, but to no purpose. Once, when he felt that he must take a trip, he undressed and went to bed. He fell asleep, and slept soundly until he heard the whistle of the midnight train. Instantly he was out of bed, and by the time they had changed engines he was at the station ready to go.

The mania for stopping trains had been equally irresistible. He would bite his lips, his fingers, but he would also stop the train.

The moment the mischief (for such it was, in nearly every instance) was done, he would suffer greatly in dread of being found out. But to-night, as on the occasion of the daylight stop in the cañon, he had no warning, no opportunity to check himself, nor any desire to do so. In each instance he had heard, dozing in the day-coach and sleeping soundly in his berth; the voice cry: "John! John!" and instantly his brain was ablaze with the light of burning wreckage. In the cañon he had only felt, indefinitely, the danger ahead; but to-night he saw the bridge swept away, and the dark gorge that yawned in front of them. Instantly upon hearing the cry that woke him, he saw it all.

"When I realized that the train was still moving, that my first effort to stop had failed, I flung these strong men from me with the greatest ease. I'm sure I should have burst those steel bands that bound my wrists if it had been necessary.

"Thank God it's all over. I feel now that I am cured,—that I can settle down contented."

The man drew a handkerchief from his pocket and wiped his forehead, keeping his face to the window for a long time.

When the conductor went forward, he found that it was as the porter had pictured. The high bridge had been carried away by a water-spout; and on the edge of the opening the engine trembled, her pilot pointing out over the black abyss.

McNally, having driven his fireman from the deck, stood in the cab gripping the air-lever and watching the pump. At that time we used what is technically known as "straight air"; so that if the pump stopped the air played out.

The conductor ordered the passengers to leave the train.

The rain had ceased, but the lightning was still playing about the summit of the range, and when it flashed, those who had gone forward saw McNally standing at his open window, looking as grand and heroic as the captain on the bridge of his sinking ship.

A nervous and somewhat thoughtless person came close under the cab to ask the engineer why he didn't back up.

There was no answer. McNally thought it must be obvious to a man with the intelligence of an oyster, that to release the brakes would be to let the heavy train shove him over the bank, even if his engine had the power to back up, which she had not.

The trainmen were working quietly, but very effectively, unloading. The day coaches had been emptied, the hand-brakes set, and all the wheels blocked with links and pins and stones, when the link between the engine and the mail-car snapped and the engine moved forward.

McNally heard the snap and felt her going, leaped from the window, caught and held a scrub cedar that grew in a rock crevice, and saw his black steed plunge down the dark cañon, a sheer two thousand feet.

McNally had been holding her in the back motion with steam in her cylinders; and now, when she leaped out into space, her throttle flew wide, a knot in the whistle-rope caught in the throttle, opening the whistle-valve as well. Down, down she plunged,—her wheels whirling in mid-air, a solid stream of fire escaping from her quivering stack, and from her throat a shriek that almost froze the blood in the veins of the onlookers. Fainter and farther came the cry, until at last the wild waters caught her, held her, hushed her, and smothered out her life.

CHASING THE WHITE MAIL

Over the walnuts and wine, as they say in Fifth Avenue, the gray-haired gentleman and I lingered long after the last of the diners had left the café car. One by one the lights were lowered. Some of the table-stewards had removed their duck and donned their street clothes. The shades were closely drawn, so that people could not peep in when the train was standing. The chief steward was swinging his punch on his finger and yawning. My venerable friend, who was a veritable author's angel, was a retired railway president with plenty of time to talk.

"We had, on the Vandalia," he began after lighting a fresh cigar, "a daredevil driver named Hubbard—'Yank' Hubbard they called him. He was a first-class mechanic, sober and industrious, but notoriously reckless, though he had never had a wreck. The Superintendent of Motive Power had selected him for the post of master-mechanic at Effingham, but I had held him up on account of his bad reputation as a wild rider.

"We had been having a lot of trouble with California fruit trains,— delays, wrecks, cars looted while in the ditch,—and I had made the delay of a fruit train almost a capital offence. The bulletin was, I presume, rather severe, and the enginemen and conductors were not taking it very well.

"One night the White Mail was standing at the station at East St. Louis (that was before the first bridge was built) loading to leave. My car was on behind, and I was walking up and down having a good smoke. As I turned near the engine, I stopped to watch the driver of the White Mail pour oil in the shallow holes on the link-lifters without wasting a drop. He was on the opposite side of the engine, and I could see only his flitting, flickering torch and the dipping, bobbing spout of his oiler.

"A man, manifestly another engineer, came up. The Mail driver lifted his torch and said, 'Hello, Yank,' to which the new-comer made no direct response. He seemed to have something on his mind. 'What are you out on?' asked the engineer, glancing at the other's overalls. 'Fast freight—perishable—must make time—no excuse will be taken,' he snapped, quoting and misquoting from my severe circular. 'Who's in that Kaskaskia?' he asked, stepping up close to the man with the torch.

"'The ol' man,' said the engineer.

"'No! ol' man, eh? Well! I'll give him a canter for his currency this trip,' said Yank, gloating. 'I'll follow him like a scandal; I'll stay with him this night like the odor of a hot box. Say, Jimmie,' he laughed, 'when that tintype of yours begins to lay down on you, just bear in mind that my pilot is under the ol' man's rear brake-beam, and that the headlight of the 99 is haunting him.'

"'Don't get gay, now,' said the engineer of the White Mail.

"'Oh, I'll make him think California fruit is not all that's perishable on the road to-night,' said Yank, hurrying away to the round-house.

"Just as we were about to pull out, our engineer, who was brother to Yank, found a broken frame and was obliged to go to the house for another locomotive. We were an hour late when we left that night, carrying signals for the fast freight. As we left the limits of the yard, Hubbard's headlight swung out on the main line, picked up two slender shafts of silver, and shot them under our rear end. The first eight or ten miles were nearly level. I sat and watched the headlight of the fast freight. He seemed to be keeping his interval until we hit the hill at Collinsville. There was hard pounding then for him for five or six miles. Just as the Kaskaskia dropped from the ridge between the east and west Silver Creek, the haunting light swept round the curve at Hagler's tank. I thought he must surely take water here; but he plunged on down the hill, coming to the surface a few minutes later on the high prairie east of Saint Jacobs.

"Highland, thirty miles out, was our first stop. We took water there; and before we could get away from the tank, Hubbard had his twin shafts of silver under my car. We got a good start here, but our catch engine proved to be badly coaled and a poor steamer. Up to this time she had done fairly well, but after the first two hours she began to lose. Seeing no more of the freight train, I turned in, not a little pleased to think that Mr. Yank's headlight would not haunt me again that trip. I fell asleep, but woke again when the train stopped, probably at Vandalia. I had just begun to doze again when our engine let out a frightful scream for brakes. I knew what that meant,—Hubbard was behind us. I let my shade go up, and saw the light of the freight train shining past me and lighting up the water-tank. I was getting a bit nervous, when I felt our train pulling out.

"Of course Hubbard had to water again; but as he had only fifteen loads, and a bigger tank, he could go as far as the Mail could without stopping. Moreover, we were bound to stop at county seats; and as often as we did so we had the life scared out of us, for there was not an air-brake freight car on the system at that time. What a night that must have been for the freight crew! They were on top constantly, but I believe the beggars enjoyed it all. Any conductor but Jim Lawn would have stopped and reported the engineer at the first telegraph station. Still, I have always had an idea that the train-master was tacitly in the conspiracy, for his bulletin had been a hot one delivered orally by the Superintendent, whom I had seen personally.

"Well, along about midnight Hubbard's headlight got so close, and kept so close, that I could not sleep. His brother, who was pulling the Mail, avoided whistling him down; for when he did he only showed that there was danger, and published his bad brother's recklessness. The result was that when the Mail screamed I invariably braced myself. I don't believe I should have stood it, only I felt it would all be over in another hour; for we should lose Yank at Effingham, the end of the freight's division. It happened, however, that there was no one to relieve him, or no engine rather; and Yank went through to Terre Haute. I was sorry, but I hated to show the white feather. I knew our fresh engine would lose him, with his tired fireman and dirty fire. Once or twice I saw his lamp, but at Longpoint we lost him for good. I went to bed again, but I could not sleep. I used to boast that I could sleep in a boiler-maker's shop; but the long dread of that fellow's pilot had unnerved me. I had wild, distressing dreams.

"The next morning, when I got to my office, I found a column of news cut from a morning paper. It had the usual scare-head, and began by announcing that the White Mail, with General Manager Blank's car Kaskaskia, came in on time, carrying signals for a freight train. The second section had not arrived, 'as we go to press.' I think I swore softly at that point. Then I read on, for there was a lot more. It seemed, the paper stated, that a gang of highwaymen had planned to rob the Mail at Longpoint, which had come to be regarded as a regular robber station. One of the robbers, being familiar with train rules, saw the signal lights on the Mail and mistook it for a special, which is often run as first section of a fast train, and they let it pass. They flagged the freight train, and one of the robbers, who was doubtless new at the business, caught the passing engine and climbed into the cab. The engineer, seeing the man's masked face at his elbow, struck it a fearful blow with his great fist. The amateur desperado sank to the floor, his big, murderous gun rattling on the iron plate of the coal-deck. Yank, the engineer, grabbed the gun, whistled off-brakes, and opened the throttle. The sudden lurch forward proved too much for a weak link, and the train parted, leaving the rest of the robbers and the train crew to fight it out. As soon as the engineer discovered that the train had parted, he slowed down and stopped.

"When he had picketed the highwayman out on the tank-deck with a piece of bell-cord, one end of which was fixed to the fellow's left foot and the other to the whistle lever, Yank set his fireman, with a white light and the robber's gun, on the rear car and flagged back to the rescue. The robbers, seeing the blunder they had made, took a few parting shots at the trainmen on the top of the train, mounted their horses, and rode away.

"When the train had coupled up again, they pulled on up to the next station, where the conductor reported the cause of delay, and from which station the account of the attempted robbery had been wired.

"I put the paper down and walked over to a window that overlooked the yards. The second section of the White Mail was coming in. As the engine rolled past, Yank looked up; and there was a devilish grin on his black face. The fireman was sitting on the fireman's seat, the gun across his lap. A young fellow, wearing a long black coat, a bell-rope, and a scared look, was sweeping up the deck.

"When I returned to my desk, the Superintendent of Motive Power was standing near it. When I sat down, he spread a paper before me. I glanced at it and recognized Yank Hubbard's appointment to the post of master-mechanic at Effingham.

"I dipped a pen in the ink-well and wrote across it in red, 'O—K.'"

OPPRESSING THE OPPRESSOR

"Is this the President's office?"

"Yes, sir."

"Can I see the President?"

"Yes,—I'm the President."

The visitor placed one big boot in a chair, hung his soft hat on his knee, dropped his elbow on the hat, let his chin fall in the hollow of his hand, and waited.

The President of the Santa Fé, leaning over a flat-topped table, wrote leisurely. When he had finished, he turned a kindly face to the visitor and asked what could be done.

"My name's Jones."

"Yes?"

"I presume you know about me,—Buffalo Jones, of Garden City."

"Well," began the President, "I know a lot of Joneses, but where is Garden City?"

"Down the road a piece, 'bout half-way between Wakefield and Turner's Tank. I want you folks to put in a switch there,—that's what I've come about. I'd like to have it in this week."

"Anybody living at Garden City?"

"Yes, all that's there's livin'."

"About how many?"

"One and a half when I'm away,—Swede and Injin."

The President of the Santa Fé smiled and rolled his lead pencil between the palms of his hands. Mr. Jones watched him and pitied him, as one watches and pities a child who is fooling with firearms. "He don't know I'm loaded," thought Jones.

"Well," said the President, "when you get your town started so that there will be some prospect of getting a little business, we shall be only too glad been seen properly, he would subside. What's the matter with your friend—Ah, here comes the Honorable gentleman now."

The President beckoned with his index finger and his friend came in. Looking him in the eye, the President asked in a stage whisper: "Have you—seen—Jones?"

"No, sir," said the Honorable gentleman. "I had no authority to see him."

"It's damphunny," said O'Marity, "if the President 'ave seen 'im, 'e don't quit."

"I certainly saw a man called Jones,—Buffalo Jones of Garden City. He wanted a side track put in half-way between Wakefield and Turner's Tank."

"And you told him, 'Certainly, we'll do it at once,'" said the General Manager.

"No," the President replied, "I told him we would not do it at once, because there was no business or prospect of business to justify the expense."

"Ah—h," said the Manager.

O'Marity whistled softly.

The Honorable gentleman smiled, and looked out through the open window to where the members of the State legislature were going up the broad steps to the State House.

"Mr. Rong," the Manager began, "it is all a horrible mistake. You have never 'seen' Jones. Not in the sense that we mean. When you see a politician or a man who herds with politicians, he is supposed to be yours,—you are supposed to have acquired a sort of interest in him,—an interest that is valued so long as the individual is in sight. You are entitled to his support and influence, up to, and including the date on which your influence expires." All the time the Manager kept jerking his thumb toward the window that held the Honorable gentleman, using the President's friend as a living example of what he was trying to explain.

"Is Jones a member?"

"No, Mr. Rong, but he controls a few members. It is easier, you understand, to acquire a drove of steers by buying a bunch than by picking them up here and there, one at a time."

"I protest," said the Honorable member, "against the reference to members of the legislature as 'cattle.'"

Neither of the railway men appeared to hear the protest.

"I think I understand now," said the President. "And I wish, Robson, you would take this matter in hand. I confess that I have no stomach for such work."

"Very well," said the Manager. "Please instruct your—your—" and he jerked his thumb toward the Honorable gentleman—"your friend to send Jones to my office."

The Honorable gentleman went white and then flushed red, but he waited for no further orders. As he strode towards the door, Robson, with a smooth, unruffled brow, but with a cold smile playing over his handsome face, with mock courtesy and a wide sweep of his open hand, waved the visitor through the open door.

"Mr. Jones wishes to see you," said the chief clerk.

"Oh, certainly—show Mr. Jones—Ah, good-morning, Mr. Jones, glad to see you. How's Garden City? Going to let us in on the ground floor, Mr. Rong tells me. Here, now, fire up; take this big chair and tell me all about your new town."

Jones took a cigar cautiously from the box. When the Manager offered him a match he lighted up gingerly, as though he expected the thing to blow up.

"Now, Mr. Jones, as I understand it, you want a side track put in at once. The matter of depot and other buildings will wait, but I want you to promise to let us have at least ten acres of ground. Perhaps it would be better to transfer that to us at once. I'll see" (the Manager pressed a button). "Send the chief engineer to me, George," as the chief clerk looked in.

All this time Jones smoked little short puffs, eyeing the Manager and his own cigar. When the chief engineer came in he was introduced to Mr. Jones, the man who was going to give Kansas the highest boom she had ever had.

While Jones stood in open-mouthed amazement, the Manager instructed the engineer to go to Garden City when it would suit Mr. Jones, lay out a siding that would hold fifty loads, and complete the job at the earliest possible moment.

"By the way, Mr. Jones, have you got transportation over our line?"

Mr. Jones managed to gasp the one word, "No."

"Buz-z-zz," went the bell. "George, make out an annual for Mr. Jones,—Comp. G.M."

Jones steadied himself by resting an elbow on the top of the Manager's desk. The chief engineer was writing in a little note-book.

"Now, Mr. Jones—ah, your cigar's out!—how much is this ten acres to cost us?—a thousand dollars, I believe you told Mr. Rong."

"Yes, I did tell him that; but if this is straight and no jolly, it ain't goin' to cost you a cent."

"Well, that's a great deal better than most towns treat us," said the Manager. "Now, Mr. Jones, you will have to excuse me; I have some business with the President. Don't fail to look in on me when you come to town; and rest assured that the Santa Fé will leave nothing undone that might help your enterprise."

With a hearty handshake the Manager, usually a little frigid and remote, passed out, leaving Mr. Jones to the tender mercies of the chief engineer.

Up to this point there is nothing unusual in this story. The remarkable part is the fact that the building of a side track in an open plain turned out to be good business. In a year's time there was a neat station and more sidings. The town boomed with a rapidity that amazed even the boomers. To be sure, it had its relapses; but still, if you look from the window as the California Limited crashes by, you will see a pretty little town when you reach the point on the time-table called

"Garden City."

THE IRON HORSE AND THE TROLLEY

I

Two prospectors had three claims in a new camp in British Columbia, but they had not the $7.50 to pay for having them recorded. They told their story to Colonel Topping, author of "The Yellowstone Park," and the Colonel advanced the necessary amount. In time the prospectors returned $5.00 of the loan, and gave the Colonel one of the claims for the balance, but more for his kindness to them; for they reckoned it a bully good prospect. Because they considered it the best claim in the camp, they called it Le Roi. Subsequently the Colonel sold this "King," that had cost him $2.50, for $30,000.00.

The new owners of Le Roi stocked the claim; and for the following two or three years, when a man owed a debt that he was unwilling to pay, he paid it in Le Roi stock. If he felt like backing a doubtful horse, he put up a handful of mining stock to punish the winner. There is in the history of this interesting mine a story of a man swapping a lot of Le Roi stock for a burro. The former owner of the donkey took the stock and the man it came from into court, declaring that the paper was worthless, and that he had been buncoed. As late as 1894, a man who ran a restaurant offered 40,000 shares of Le Roi stock for four barrels of Canadian whiskey; but the whiskey man would not trade that way.

In the meantime, however, men were working in the mine; and now they began to ship ore. It was worth $27.00 a ton, and the stock became valuable. Scattered over the Northwest were 500,000 shares that were worth $500,000.00. Nearly all the men who had put money into the enterprise were Yankees,—mining men from Spokane, just over the border. These men began now to pick up all the stray shares that could be found; and in a little while eight-tenths of the shares were held by men living south of the line. At Northport, in Washington, they built one of the finest smelters in the Northwest, hauled their ore over there, and smelted it. The ore was rich in gold and copper. They put in a 300 horse-power hoisting-engine and a 40-drill air-compressor,—the largest in Canada,—taking all the money for these improvements out of the mine. The thing was a success, and news of it ran down to Chicago. A party of men with money started for the new gold fields, but as they were buying tickets three men rushed in and took tickets for Seattle. These were mining men; and those who had bought only to British Columbia cashed in, asked for transportation to the coast, and followed the crowd to the Klondike.

In that way Le Roi for the moment was forgotten.

II

The Lieutenant-Governor of the Northwest Territories, who had been a journalist and had a nose for news, heard of the new camp. All the while men were rushing to the Klondike, for it is the nature of man to go from home for a thing that he might secure under his own vine.

The Governor visited the new camp. A man named Ross Thompson had staked out a town at the foot of Le Roi dump and called it Rossland. The Governor put men to work quietly in the mine and then went back to his plank palace at Regina, capital of the Northwest Territories,—to a capital that looked for all the world like a Kansas frontier town that had just ceased to be the county seat. Here for months he waited, watching the "Imperial Limited" cross the prairie, receiving delegations of half-breeds and an occasional report from one of the common miners in Le Roi. If a capitalist came seeking a soft place to invest, the Governor pointed to the West-bound Limited and whispered in the stranger's ear. To all letters of inquiry coming from Ottawa or England,—letters from men who wanted to be told where to dig for gold,—he answered, "Klondike."

By and by the Governor went to Rossland again. The mine, of which he owned not a single share of stock, was still producing. When he left Rossland he knew all about the lower workings, the value and extent of the ore body.

By this time nearly all the Le Roi shares were held by Spokane people. The Governor, having arranged with a wealthy English syndicate, was in a position to buy the mine; but the owners did not seem anxious to sell. Eventually, however, when he was able to offer them an average of $7.50 for shares that had cost the holders but from ten to sixty cents a share, about half of them were willing to sell; the balance were not. Now the Governor cared nothing for this "balance" so long as he could secure a majority,—a controlling interest in the mine,—for the English would have it in no other way. A few thousand scattering shares he had already picked

SNOW ON THE HEADLIGHT

up, and now, from the faction who were willing to sell, he secured an option on 242,000 shares, which, together with the odd shares already secured, would put his friends in control of the property.

As news of the proposed sale got out, the gorge that was yawning between the two factions grew wider.

Finally, when the day arrived for the transfer to be made, the faction opposed to the sale prepared to make trouble for those who were selling, to prevent the moving of the seal of the company to Canada—in short, to stop the sale. They did not go with guns to the secretary and keeper of the seal and say, "Bide where ye be"; but they went into court and swore out warrants for the arrest of the secretary and those of the directors who favored the sale, charging them with conspiracy.

It was midnight in Spokane.

A black locomotive, hitched to a dark day-coach, stood in front of the Great Northern station. The dim light of the gauge lamp showed two nodding figures in the cab. Out on the platform a man walked up and down, keeping an eye on the engine, that was to cost him a cool $1000.00 for a hundred-mile run. Presently a man with his coat-collar about his ears stepped up into the gangway, shook the driver, and asked him where he was going.

"Goin' to sleep."

The man would not be denied, however, and when he became too pressing, the driver got up and explained that the cab of his engine was his castle, and made a move with his right foot.

"Hold," cried his tormentor, "do you know that you are about to lay violent hands upon an officer o' the law?"

"No," said the engineer, "but I'll lay a violent foot up agin the crown-sheet o' your trousers if you don't jump."

The man jumped.

Now the chief despatcher came from the station, stole along the shadow side of the car, and spoke to the man who had ordered the train.

A deputy sheriff climbed up on the rear end of the special, tried the door, shaded his eyes, and endeavored to look into the car.

"Have you the running orders?" asked the man who was paying for the entertainment.

"Yes."

"Let her go, then."

All this was in a low whisper; and now the despatcher climbed up on the fireman's side and pressed a bit of crumpled tissue-paper into the driver's hand.

"Pull out over the switches slowly, and when you are clear of the yards read your orders an' fly."

The driver opened the throttle gently, the big wheels began to revolve, and the next moment the sheriff and one of his deputies boarded the engine. They demanded to know where that train was bound for.

"The train," said the driver, tugging at the throttle, "is back there at the station. I'm goin' to the round-house."

When the sheriff, glancing back, saw that the coach had been cut off, he swung himself down.

"They've gi'n it up," said the deputy.

"I reckon—what's that?" said the sheriff. It was the wild, long whistle of the lone black engine just leaving the yards. The two officers faced each other and stood listening to the flutter of the straight stack of the black racer as she responded to the touch of the erstwhile drowsy driver, who was at that moment laughing at the high sheriff, and who would return to tell of it, and gloat in the streets of Spokane.

The sheriff knew that three of the men for whom he held warrants were at Hillier, seven miles on the way to Canada. This engine, then, had been sent to pick them up and bear them away over the border. An electric line paralleled the steam way to Hillier, and now the sheriff boarded a trolley and set sail to capture the engine, leaving one deputy to guard the special car.

By the time the engineer got the water worked out of his cylinders, the trolley was creeping up beside his tank. He saw the flash from the wire above as the car, nodding and dipping like a light boat in the wake of a ferry, shot beneath the cross-wires, and knew instantly that she was after him.

An electric car would not be ploughing through the gloom at that rate, without a ray of light, merely for the fun of the thing. A smile of contempt curled the lip of the driver as he cut the reverse-lever back to the first notch, put on the injector, and opened the throttle yet a little wider.

The two machines were running almost neck and neck now. The trolley cried, hissed, and spat fire in her mad effort to pass the locomotive. A few stray sparks went out of the engine-stack, and fell upon the roof of the racing car. At intervals of half a minute the fireman opened the furnace door; and by the flare of light from the white-hot fire-box the engine-driver could see the men on the teetering trolley,—the motor-man, the conductor, the sheriff, and his deputy.

Slowly now the black flier began to slip away from the electric machine.

The driver, smiling across the glare of the furnace door at his silent, sooty companion, touched the throttle again; and the great engine drew away from the trolley, as a jack-rabbit who has been fooling with a yellow dog passes swiftly out of reach of his silly yelp.

Now the men on the trolley heard the wild, triumphant scream of the iron horse whistling for Hillier. The three directors of Le Roi had been warned by wire, and were waiting, ready to board the engine.

The big wheels had scarcely stopped revolving when the men began to get on. They had barely begun to turn again when the trolley dashed into Hillier. The sheriff leaped to the ground and came running for the engine. The wheels slipped; and each passing second brought the mighty hand of the law, now outstretched, still nearer to the tail of the tank. She was moving now, but the sheriff was doing better. Ten feet separated the pursued and the pursuer. She slipped again, and the sheriff caught the corner of the engine-tank. By this time the driver had got the sand running; and now, as the wheels held the rail, the big engine bounded forward, almost shaking the sheriff loose. With each turn of the wheels the speed was increasing. The sheriff held on; and in three or four seconds he was taking only about two steps between telegraph poles, and then—he let go.

II

While the locomotive and the trolley were racing across the country the Governor, who was engineering it all, invested another thousand. He ordered another engine, and when she backed onto the coach the deputy sheriff told the driver that he must not leave the station. The engineer held his torch high above his head, looked the deputy over, and then went on oiling his engine. In the meantime the Governor had stored his friends away in the dark coach, including the secretary with the company's great seal. Now the deputy became uneasy.

He dared not leave the train to send a wire to his chief at Hillier, for the sheriff had said, "Keep your eye on the car."

The despatcher, whose only interest in the matter was to run the trains and earn money for his employer, having given written and verbal orders to the engineer, watched his chance and, when the sheriff was pounding on the rear door, dodged in at the front, signalling with the bell-rope to the driver to go. Frantically now the deputy beat upon the rear door of the car, but the men within only laughed as the wheels rattled over the last switch and left the lights of Spokane far behind.

Away they went over a new and crooked track, the sand and cinders sucking in round the tail of the train to torment the luckless deputy. Away over hills and rills, past Hillier, where the sheriff still stood staring down the darkness after the vanishing engine; over switches and through the Seven Devils, while the unhappy deputy hung to the rear railing with one hand and crossed himself.

Each passing moment brought the racing train still nearer the border,— to that invisible line that marks the end of Yankeeland and the beginning of the British possessions. The sheriff knew this and beat loudly upon the car door with an iron gun. The Governor let the sash fall at the top of the door and spoke, or rather yelled, to the deputy.

To the Governor's amazement, the sheriff pushed the bottle aside. Dry and dusty as he was, he would not drink. He was too mad to swallow. He poked his head into the dark coach and ordered the whole party to surrender.

"Just say what you want," said a voice in the gloom, "and we'll pass it out to you."

The sheriff became busy with some curves and reverse curves now, and made no reply.

Presently the Governor came to the window in the rear door again and called up the sheriff.

"We are now nearing the border," he said to the man on the platform. "They won't know you over there. Here you stand for law and order, and I respect you, though I don't care to meet you personally; but over the border you'll only stand for your sentence,—two years for carrying a cannon on your hip,—and then they'll take you away to prison."

The sheriff made no answer.

"Now we're going to slow down at the line to about twenty miles an hour, more or less; and if you'll take a little friendly advice, you'll fall off."

The train was still running at a furious pace. The whistle sounded,—one long, wild scream,—and the speed of the train slackened.

"Here you are," the Governor called, and the sheriff stood on the lower step.

The door opened and the Governor stepped out on the platform, followed by his companions.

"I arrest you," the sheriff shouted, "all of you."

"But you can't,—you're in British Columbia," the men laughed.

"Let go, now," said the Governor, and a moment later the deputy picked himself up and limped back over the border.

IN THE BLACK CAÑON

One Christmas, at least, will live long in the memory of the men and women who hung up their stockings at La Veta Hotel in Gunnison in 18—. Ah, those were the best days of Colorado. Then folks were brave and true to the traditions of Red Hoss Mountain, when "money flowed like liquor," and coal strikes didn't matter, for the people all had something to burn.

The Yankee proprietor of the dining-stations on this mountain line had made them as famous almost as the Harvey houses on the Santa Fé were; which praise is pardonable, since the Limited train with its café car has closed them all.

But the best of the bunch was La Veta, and the presiding genius was Nora O'Neal, the lady manager. Many an R. & W. excursionist reading this story will recall her smile, her great gray eyes, her heaps of dark brown hair, and the mountain trout that her tables held.

It will be remembered that at that time the main lines of the Rio Grande lay by the banks of the Gunnison, through the Black Cañon, over Cerro Summit, and down the Uncompaghre and the Grande to Grand Junction, the gate of the Utah Desert.

John Cassidy was an express messenger whose run was over this route and whose heart and its secret were in the keeping of Nora O'Neal.

From day to day, from week to week, he had waited her answer, which was to come to him "by Christmas."

And now, as only two days remained, he dreaded it, as he had hoped and prayed for it since the aspen leaves began to gather their gold. He knew by the troubled look she wore when off her guard that Nora was thinking.

Most of the men who were gunning in Gunnison in the early 80's were fearless men, who, when a difference of opinion arose, faced each other and fought it out; but there had come to live at La Veta a thin, quiet, handsome fellow, who moved mysteriously in and out of the camp, slept a lot by day, and showed a fondness for faro by night. When a name was needed he signed "Buckingham." His icy hand was soft and white, and his clothes fitted him faultlessly. He was handsome, and when he paid his bill at the end of the fourth week he proposed to Nora O'Neal. He was so fairer, physically, than Cassidy and so darker, morally, that Nora could not make up her mind at all, at all.

In the shadow time, between sunset and gas-light, on the afternoon of the last day but one before Christmas, Buck, as he came to be called, leaned over the office counter and put a folded bit of white paper in Nora's hand, saying, as he closed her fingers over it: "Put this powder in Cassidy's cup." He knew Cassidy merely as the messenger whose freight he coveted, and not as a contestant for Nora's heart and hand,—a hand he prized, however, as he would a bob-tailed flush, but no more.

As for Cassidy, he would be glad, waking, to find himself alive; and if this plan miscarried, Buck should be able to side-step the gallows. Anyway, dope was preferable to death.

Nora opened her hand, and in utter amazement looked at the paper. Some one interrupted them. Buck turned away, and Nora shoved the powder down deep into her jacket pocket, feeling vaguely guilty.

No. 7, the Salt Lake Limited, was an hour late that night. The regular dinner (we called it supper then) was over when Shanley whistled in.

As the headlight of the Rockaway engine gleamed along the hotel windows, Nora went back to see that everything was ready.

In the narrow passage between the kitchen and the dining-room she met Buckingham. "What are you doing here?" she demanded.

"Now, my beauty," said Buck, laying a cold hand on her arm, "don't be excited."

She turned her honest eyes to him and he almost visibly shrank from them, as she had shuddered at the strange, cold touch of his hand.

"Put that powder in Cassidy's cup," he said, and in the half-light of the little hallway she saw his cruel smile.

"And kill Cassidy, the best friend I have on earth?"

"It will not kill him, but it may save his life. I shall be in his car to-night. Sabe? Do as I tell you. He will only fall asleep for a little while, otherwise—well, he may oversleep himself." She would have passed on, but he stayed her. "Where is it?" he demanded, with a meaning glance.

She touched her jacket pocket, and he released his hold on her arm.

The shuffle and scuffle of the feet of hungry travellers who were piling into the dining-room had disturbed them. Nora passed on to the rear, Buck out to sit down and dine with the passengers, who always had a shade the best of the bill.

From his favorite seat, facing the audience, he watched the trainmen tumbling into the alcove off the west wing, in one corner of which a couple of Pullman porters in blue and gold sat at a small table, feeding with their forks and behaving better than some of their white comrades behaved.

Cassidy came in a moment later, sat down, and looked over to see if his rival was in his accustomed place. The big messenger looked steadily at the other man, who had never guessed the messenger's secret, and the other man looked down.

Already his supper, steaming hot, stood before him, while the table-girl danced attendance for the tip she was always sure of at the finish. She studied his tastes and knew his wants, from rare roast down to the small, black coffee with which he invariably concluded his meal.

When Buck looked up again he saw Nora approach the table, smile at Cassidy, and put a cup of coffee down by his plate.

The trainmen were soon through with their supper, being notoriously rapid feeders,—which disastrous habit they acquire while on freight, when they are expected to eat dinner and do an hour's switching in twenty minutes.

Unusually early for him, Buck passed out. Nora purposely avoided him, but watched him from the unlighted little private office. She saw him light a cigar and stroll down the long platform. At the rear of the last Pullman he threw his cigar away and crossed quickly to the shadow side of the train. She saw him pass along, for there were no vestibules then, and made no doubt he was climbing into Cassidy's car. As the messenger reached for his change, the cashier-manager caught his hand, drew it across the counter, leaned toward him, saying excitedly: "Be careful to-night, John; don't fall asleep or nod for a moment. Oh, be careful!" she repeated, with ever-increasing intensity, her hot hand trembling on his great wrist; "be careful, come back safe, and you shall have your answer."

When Cassidy came back to earth he was surrounded by half a dozen good-natured passengers, men and women, who had come out of the dining-room during the ten or fifteen seconds he had spent in Paradise.

A swift glance at the faces about told him that they had seen, another at Nora that she was embarrassed; but in two ticks of the office clock he protected her, as he would his safe; for his work and time had trained him to be ready instantly for any emergency.

"Good-night, sister," he called cheerily, as he hurried toward the door.

"Good-night, John," said Nora, glancing up from the till, radiant with the excitement of her "sweet distress."

"Oh, by Jove!" said a man.

"Huh!" said a woman, and they looked like people who had just missed a boat.

With her face against the window, Nora watched the red lights on the rear of No. 7 swing out to the main line.

Closing the desk, she climbed to her room on the third floor and knelt by the window. Away out on the shrouded vale she saw the dark train creeping, a solid stream of fire flowing from the short stack of the "shotgun"; for Peasley was pounding her for all she was worth in an honest effort to make up the hour that Shanley had lost in the snowdrifts of Marshall Pass. Presently she heard the muffled roar of the train on a trestle, and a moment later saw the Salt Lake Limited swallowed by the Black Cañon, in whose sunless gorges many a driver died before the scenery settled after having been disturbed by the builders of the road.

Over ahead in his quiet car Cassidy sat musing, smoking, and wondering why Nora should seem so anxious about him. Turning, he glanced about. Everything looked right, but the girl's anxiety bothered him.

Picking up a bundle of way-bills, he began checking up. The engine screamed for Sapinero, and a moment later he felt the list as they rounded Dead Man's Curve.

Unless they were flagged, the next stop would be at Cimarron, at the other end of the cañon.

His work done, the messenger lighted his pipe, settled himself in his high-backed canvas camp-chair, and put his feet up on his box for a good smoke. He tried to think of a number of things that had nothing whatever to do with Nora, but somehow she invariably elbowed into his thoughts.

He leaned over and opened his box—not the strong-box, but the wooden, trunk-like box that holds the messenger's street-coat when he's on duty and his jumper when he's off. On the under side of the lifted lid he had fixed a large panel picture of Nora O'Neal.

Buckingham, peering over a piano-box, behind which he had hidden at Gunnison, saw and recognized the photograph; for the messenger's white light stood on the little safe near the picture. For half an hour he had been watching Cassidy, wondering why he did not fall asleep. He had seen Nora put the cup down with her own hand, to guard, as he thought, against the possibility of a mistake. What will a woman not dare and do for the man she loves? He sighed softly. He recalled now that he had always exercised a powerful influence over women,—that is, the few he had known,—but he was surprised that this consistent Catholic girl should be so "dead easy."

"And now look at this one hundred and ninety-eight pounds of egotism sitting here smiling on the likeness of the lady who has just dropped bug-dust in his coffee. It's positively funny."

Such were the half-whispered musings of the would-be robber.

He actually grew drowsy waiting for Cassidy to go to sleep. The car lurched on a sharp curve, dislodging some boxes. Buck felt a strange, tingling sensation in his fingers and toes. Presently he nodded.

Cassidy sat gazing on the pictured face that had hovered over him in all his dreams for months, and as he gazed, seemed to feel her living presence. He rose as if to greet her, but kept his eyes upon the picture.

Suddenly realizing that something was wrong in his end of the car, Buck stood up, gripping the top of the piano-box. The scream of the engine startled him. The car crashed over the switch-frog at Curecanti, and Curecanti's Needle stabbed the starry vault above. The car swayed strangely and the lights grew dim.

Suddenly the awful truth flashed through his bewildered brain.

"O-o-o-oh, the wench!" he hissed, pulling his guns.

Cassidy, absorbed in the photo, heard a door slam; and it came to him instantly that Nora had boarded the train at Gunnison, and that some one was showing her over to the head end. As he turned to meet her, he saw Buck staggering toward him, holding a murderous gun in each hand. Instantly he reached for his revolver, but a double flash from the guns of the enemy blinded him and put out the bracket-lamps. As the messenger sprang forward to find his foe, the desperado lunged against him. Cassidy grabbed him, lifted him bodily, and smashed him to the floor of the car; but with the amazing tenacity and wonderful agility of the trained gun-fighter, Buck managed to fire as he fell. The big bullet grazed the top of Cassidy's head, and he fell unconscious across the half-dead desperado.

Buck felt about for his gun, which had fallen from his hand; but already the "bug-dust" was getting in its work. Sighing heavily, he joined the messenger in a quiet sleep.

At Cimarron they broke the car open, revived the sleepers, restored the outlaw to the Ohio State Prison, from which he had escaped, and the messenger to Nora O'Neal.

JACK RAMSEY'S REASON

When Bill Ross romped up over the range and blew into Edmonton in the wake of a warm chinook, bought tobacco at the Hudson's Bay store, and began to regale the gang with weird tales of true fissures, paying placers, and rich loads lying "virgin," as he said, in Northern British Columbia, the gang accepted his tobacco and stories for what they were worth; for it is a tradition up there that all men who come in with the Mudjekeewis are liars.

That was thirty years ago.

The same chinook winds that wafted Bill Ross and his rose-hued romances into town have winged them, and the memory of them, away.

In the meantime Ross reformed, forgot, the people forgave and made him Mayor of Edmonton.

When Jack Ramsey called at the capital of British Columbia and told of a territory in that great Province where the winter winds blew warm, where snow fell only once in a while and was gone again with the first peep of the sun; of a mountain-walled wonderland between the Coast Range and the Rockies, where flowers bloomed nine months in the year and gold could be panned on almost any of the countless rivers, men said he had come down from Alaska, and that he lied.

To be sure, they did not say that to Jack,—they only telegraphed it one to another over their cigars in the club. Some of them actually believed it, and one man who had made money in California and later in Leadville said he knew it was so; for, said he, "Jack Ramsey never says or does a thing without a 'reason.'"

At the end of a week this English-bred Yankee had organized the "Chinook Mining and Milling Company, Limited."

This man was at the head of the scheme, with Jack Ramsey as Managing Director.

Ramsey was a prospector by nature made proficient by practice. He had prospected in every mining camp from Mexico to Moose Factory. If he were to find a real bonanza, his English-American friend used to say, he would be miserable for the balance of his days, or rather his to-morrows. He lived in his to-morrows,—in these and in dreams. He loved women, wine, and music, and the laughter of little children; but better than all these he loved the wilderness and the wildflowers and the soft, low singing of mountain rills. He loved the flowers of the North, for they were all sweet and innocent. On all the two thousand five hundred miles of the Yukon, he used to say, there is not one poisonous plant; and he reasoned that the plants of the Peace and the Pine and the red roses of the Upper Athabasca would be the same.

And so, one March morning, he sailed up the Sound to enter his mountain-walled wonderland by the portal of Port Simpson, which opens on the Pacific. His English-American friend went up as far as Simpson, and when the little coast steamer poked her prow into Work Channel he touched the President of the Chinook Mining and Milling Company and said, "The Gateway to God's world."

The head of the C.M. & M. Company was not surprised when Christmas came ahead of Jack Ramsey's preliminary report. Jack was a careful, conservative prospector, and would not send a report unless there was a good and substantial reason for writing it out.

In the following summer a letter came,—an extremely short one, considering what it contained; for it told, tersely, of great prospects in the wonderland. It closed with a request for a new rifle, some garden-seeds, and an H.B. letter of credit for five hundred dollars.

After a warm debate among the directors it was agreed the goods should go.

The following summer—that is, the second summer in the life of the Chinook Company—Dawson dawned on the world. That year about half the floating population of the Republic went to Cuba and the other half to the Klondike.

As the stream swelled and the channel between Vancouver Island and the mainland grew black with boats, the President of the C.M. & M. Company began to pant for Ramsey, that he might join the rush to the North. That exciting summer died and another dawned, with no news from Ramsey.

When the adventurous English-American could withstand the strain no longer, he shipped for Skagway himself. He dropped off at Port Simpson and inquired about Ramsey.

Yes, the Hudson people said, it was quite probable that Ramsey had passed in that way. Some hundreds of prospectors had gone in during the past three years, but the current created by the Klondike rush had drawn most of them out and up the Sound.

One man declared that he had seen Ramsey ship for Skagway on the "Dirigo," and, after a little help and a few more drinks, gave a minute description of a famous nugget pin which the passing pilgrim said the prospector wore.

And so the capitalist took the next boat for Skagway.

By the time he reached Dawson the death-rattle had begun to assert itself in the bosom of the boom. The most diligent inquiry failed to reveal the presence of the noted prospector. On the contrary, many old-timers from Colorado and California declared that Ramsey had never reached the Dike—that is, not since the boom. In a walled tent on a shimmering sandbar at the mouth of the crystal Klondike, Captain Jack Crawford, the "Poet Scout," severely sober in that land of large thirsts, wearing his old-time halo of lady-like behavior and hair, was conducting an "Ice Cream Emporium and Soft-drink Saloon."

"No," said the scout, with the tips of his tapered fingers trembling on an empty table, straining forward and staring into the stranger's face; "no, Jack Ramsey has not been here; and if what you say be true—he sleeps alone in yonder fastness. Alas, poor Ramsey!—Ah knew 'im well"; and he sank on a seat, shaking with sobs.

The English-American, on his way out, stopped at Simpson again. From a half-breed trapper he heard of a white man who had crossed the Coast Range three grasses ago. This white man had three or four head of cattle, a Cree servant, and a queer-looking cayuse with long ears and a mournful, melancholy cry. This latter member of the gang carried the outfit.

Taking this half-caste Cree to guide him, the mining man set out in search of the long-lost Ramsey. They crossed the first range and searched the streams north of the Peace River pass, almost to the crest of the continent, but found no trace of the prospector.

When the summer died and the wilderness was darkened by the Northern night, the search was abandoned.

The years drifted into the past, and finally the Chinook Mining and Milling Company went to the wall. The English-American promoter, smarting under criticism, reimbursed each of his associates and took over the office, empty ink-stands and blotting paper, and so blotted out all records of the one business failure of his life.

But he could not blot out Jack Ramsey from his memory. There was a "reason," he would say, for Ramsey's silence.

One day, when in Edmonton, he met Mayor Ross, who had come into the country by the back door some thirty years ago. The tales coaxed from the Mayor's memory corresponded with Ramsey's report; and having nothing but time and money, the ex-President of the C.M. & M. Company determined to go in via the Peace River pass and see for himself. He made the acquaintance of Smith "The Silent," as he was called, who was at that time pathfinding for the Grand Trunk Pacific, and secured permission to go in with the engineers.

At Little Slave Lake he picked up Jim Cromwell, a free-trader, who engaged to guide the mining man into the wonderland he had described.

The story of Ramsey and his rambles appealed to Cromwell, who talked tirelessly, and to the engineer, who listened long; and in time the habitants of Cromwell's domains, which covered a country some seven hundred miles square, all knew the story and all joined in the search.

Beyond the pass of the Peace an old Cree caught up with them and made signs, for he was deaf and dumb. But strange as it may seem, somehow, somewhere, he had heard the story of the lost miner and knew that this strange white man was the miner's friend.

Long he sat by the camp fire, when the camp was asleep, trying, by counting on his fingers and with sticks, to make Cromwell understand what was on his mind.

When day dawned, he plucked Cromwells' sleeve, then walked away fifteen or twenty steps, stopped, unrolled his blankets, and lay down, closing his eyes as if asleep. Presently he got up, rubbed his eyes, lighted his pipe, smoked for awhile, then knocked the fire out on a stone. Then he got up, stamped the fire out as though it had been a camp fire, rolled up his blankets, and travelled on down the slope some twenty feet and repeated the performance. On the next march he made but ten feet. He stopped, put his pack down, seated himself on the trunk of a fallen tree and, with his back to Cromwell, began gesticulating, as if talking to some one, nodding and shaking his head. Then he got a pick and began digging.

At the end of an hour Cromwell and the engineer had agreed that these stations were day's marches and the rests camping places. In short, it was two and a half "sleeps" to what he wanted to show them,—a prospect, a gold mine maybe,—and so Cromwell and the English-American detached themselves and set out at the heels of the mute Cree in search of something.

On the morning of the third day the old Indian could scarcely control himself, so eager was he to be off.

All through the morning the white men followed him in silence. Noon came, and still the Indian pushed on.

At two in the afternoon, rounding the shoulder of a bit of highland overlooking a beautiful valley, they came suddenly upon a half-breed boy playing with a wild goose that had been tamed.

Down in the valley a cabin stood, and over the valley a small drove of cattle were grazing.

Suddenly from behind the hogan came the weird wail of a Colorado canary, who would have been an ass in Absalom's time.

They asked the half-breed boy his name, and he shook his head. They asked for his father, and he frowned.

The mute old Indian took up a pick, and they followed him up the slope. Presently he stopped at a stake upon which they could still read the faint pencil-marks:—

C.M.

M. Co.

L't'd

The old Indian pointed to the ground with an expression which looked to the white men like an interrogation. Cromwell nodded, and the Indian began to dig. Cromwell brought a shovel, and they began sinking a shaft.

The English-American, with a sickening, sinking sensation, turned toward the cabin. The boy preceded him and stood in the door. The man put his hand on the boy's head and was about to enter when he caught sight of a nugget at the boy's neck. He stooped and lifted it. The boy shrank back, but the man, going deadly pale, clutched the child, dragging the nugget from his neck.

Now all the Indian in the boy's savage soul asserted itself, and he fought like a little demon. Pitying the child in its impotent rage, the man gave him the nugget and turned away.

Across the valley an Indian woman came walking rapidly, her arms full of turnips and onions and other garden-truck. The white man looked and loathed her; for he felt confident that Ramsey had been murdered, his trinkets distributed, and his carcass cast to the wolves.

When the boy ran to meet the woman, the white man knew by his behavior that he was her child. When the boy had told his mother how the white man had behaved, she flew into a rage, dropped her vegetables, dived into the cabin, and came out with a rifle in her hands. To her evident surprise the man seemed not to dread death, but stood staring at the rifle, which he recognized as the rifle he had sent to Ramsey. To his surprise she did not shoot, but uttering a strange cry, started up the slope, taking the gun with her. With rifle raised and flashing eyes she ordered the two men out of the prospect hole. Warlike as she seemed, she was more than welcome, for she was a woman and could talk. She talked Cree, of course, but it sounded good to Cromwell. Side by side the handsome young athlete and the Cree woman sat and exchanged stories.

Half an hour later the Englishman came up and asked what the prospect promised.

"Ah," said Cromwell, sadly, "this is another story. There is no gold in this vale, though from what this woman tells me the hills are full of it. However," he added, "I believe we have found your friend."

"Yes?" queried the capitalist.

"Yes," echoed Cromwell, "here are his wife and his child; and here, where we're grubbing, his grave."

"Quite so, quite so," said the big, warm-hearted English-American, glaring at the ground; "and that was Ramsey's 'reason' for not writing."

THE GREAT WRECK ON THE PÈRE MARQUETTE

The reader is not expected to believe this red tale; but if he will take the trouble to write the General Manager of the Père Marquette Railroad, State of Michigan, U.S.A. enclosing stamped envelope for answer, I make no doubt that good man, having by this time recovered from the dreadful shock occasioned by the wreck, will cheerfully verify the story even to the minutest detail.

Of course Kelly, being Irish, should have been a Democrat; but he was not. He was not boisterously or offensively Republican, but he was going to vote the prosperity ticket. He had tried it four years ago, and business had never been better on the Père Marquette. Moreover, he had a new hand-car.

The management had issued orders to the effect that there must be no coercion of employees. It was pretty well understood among the men that the higher officials would vote the Republican ticket and leave the little fellows free to do the same. So Kelly, being boss of the gang, could not, with "ju" respect to the order of the Superintendent, enter into the argument going on constantly between Burke and Shea on one side and Lucien Boseaux, the French-Canadian-Anglo-Saxon-Foreign-American Citizen, on the other. This argument always reached its height at noon-time, and had never been more heated than now, it being the day before election.

"Here is prosper tee," laughed Lucien, holding up a half-pint bottle of vin rouge.

"Yes," Burke retorted, "an' ye have four pound of cotton waste in the bottom o' that buckct to trow the grub t' the top. Begad, I'd vote for O'Bryan wid an empty pail—er none at all—before I'd be humbugged."

"Un I," said Lucien, "would pour Messieur Rousveau vote if my baskett shall all the way up be cotton."

"Sure ye would," said Shea, "and ate the cotton too, ef your masther told ye to. 'Tis the likes of ye, ye bloomin' furreighner, that kapes the thrust alive in this country."

When they were like to come to blows, Kelly, with a mild show of superiority, which is second nature to a section boss, would interfere and restore order. All day they worked and argued, lifting low joints and lowering high centres; and when the red sun sank in the tree-tops, filtering its gold through the golden leaves, they lifted the car onto the rails and started home.

When the men had mounted, Lucien at the forward handle and Burke and Shea side by side on the rear bar, they waited impatiently for Kelly to light his pipe and seat himself comfortably on the front of the car, his heels hanging near to the ties.

There was no more talk now. The men were busy pumping, the "management" inspecting the fish-plates, the culverts, and, incidentally, watching the red sun slide down behind the trees.

At the foot of a long slope, down which the men had been pumping with all their might, there was a short bridge. The forest was heavy here, and already the shadow of the woods lay over the right-of-way. As the car reached the farther end of the culvert, the men were startled by a great explosion. The hand-car was lifted bodily and thrown from the track.

The next thing Lucien remembers is that he woke from a fevered sleep, fraught with bad dreams, and felt warm water running over his chest. He put his hand to his shirt-collar, removed it, and found it red with blood. Thoroughly alarmed, he got to his feet and looked, or rather felt, himself over. His fingers found an ugly ragged gash in the side of his neck, and the fear and horror of it all dazed him.

He reeled and fell again, but this time did not lose consciousness.

Finally, when he was able to drag himself up the embankment to where the car hung crosswise on the track, the sight he saw was so appalling he forgot his own wounds.

On the side opposite to where he had fallen, Burke and Shea lay side by side, just as they had walked and worked and fought for years, and just as they would have voted on the morrow had they been spared. Immediately in front of the car, his feet over one rail and his neck across the other, lay the mortal remains of Kelly the boss, the stub of his black pipe still sticking between his teeth. As Lucien stooped to lift the helpless head his own blood, spurting from the wound in his neck, flooded the face and covered the clothes of the limp foreman. Finding no signs of life in the section boss, the wounded, and by this time thoroughly frightened, French-Canadian turned his attention to the other two victims. Swiftly now the realization of the awful tragedy came over the wounded man. His first thought was of the express now nearly due. With a great effort he succeeded in placing the car on the rails, and then began the work of loading the dead. Out of respect for the office so lately filled by Kelly, he was lifted first and placed on the front of the car, his head pillowed on Lucien's coat. Next he put Burke aboard, bleeding profusely the while; and then began the greater task of loading Shea. Shea was a heavy man, and by the time Lucien had him aboard he was ready to faint from exhaustion and the loss of blood.

Now he must pump up over the little hill; for if the express should come round the curve and fall down the grade, the hand-car would be in greater danger than ever.

After much hard work he gained the top of the hill, the hot blood spurting from his neck at each fall of the handle-bar, and went hurrying down the long easy grade to Charlevoix.

To show how the trifles of life will intrude at the end, it is interesting to hear Lucien declare that one of the first thoughts that came to him on seeing the three prostrate figures was, that up to that moment the wreck had worked a Republican gain of one vote, with his own in doubt.

But now he had more serious work for his brain, already reeling from exhaustion. At the end of fifteen minutes he found himself hanging onto the handle, more to keep from falling than for any help he was giving the car. The evening breeze blowing down the slope helped him, so that the car was really losing nothing in speed. He dared not relax his hold; for if his strength should give out and the car stop, the express would come racing down through the twilight and scoop him into eternity. So he toiled on, dazed, stupefied, fighting for life, surrounded by the dead.

Presently above the singing of the wheels he heard a low sound, like a single, smothered cough of a yard engine suddenly reversed. Now he had the feeling of a man flooded with ice-water, so chilled was his blood. Turning his head to learn the cause of delay (he had fancied the pilot of an engine under his car), he saw Burke, one of the dead men, leap up and glare into his face. That was too much for Lucien, weak as he was, and twisting slightly, he sank to the floor of the car.

Slowly Burke's wandering reason returned. Seeing Shea at his feet, bloodless and apparently unhurt, he kicked him, gently at first, and then harder, and Shea stood up. Mechanically the waking man took his place by Burke's side and began pumping, Lucien lying limp between them. Kelly, they reasoned, must have been dead some time, by the way he was pillowed.

When Shea was reasonably sure that he was alive, he looked at his mate.

"Phat way ar're ye feelin'?" asked Burke.

"Purty good fur a corpse. How's yourself?"

"Oh, so-so!"

"Th' Lord is good to the Irish."

"But luck ut poor Kelly."

"'Tis too bad," said Shea, "an' him dyin' a Republican."

"'Tis the way a man lives he must die."

"Yes," said Shea, thoughtfully, "thim that lives be the sword must go be the board."

When they had pumped on silently for awhile, Shea asked, "How did ye load thim, Burke?"

"Why—I—I suppose I lifted them aboard. I had no derrick."

"Did ye lift me, Burke?"

"I'm damned if I know, Shea," said Burke, staring ahead, for Kelly had moved. "Keep her goin'," he added, and then he bent over the prostrate foreman. He lifted Kelly's head, and the eyes opened. He raised the head a little higher, and Kelly saw the blood upon his beard, on his coat, on his hands.

"Are yez hurted, Kelly?" he asked.

"Hurted! Man, I'm dyin'. Can't you see me heart's blood ebbin' over me?" And then Burke, crossing himself, laid the wounded head gently down again.

By this time they were nearing their destination. Burke, seeing Lucien beyond human aid, took hold again and helped pump, hoping to reach Charlevoix in time to secure medical aid, or a priest at least, for Kelly.

When the hand-car stopped in front of the station at Charlevoix, the employees watching, and the prospective passengers waiting, for the express train gathered about the car.

"Get a docther!" shouted Burke, as the crowd closed in on them.

In a few moments a man with black whiskers, a small hand-grip, and bicycle trousers panted up to the crowd and pushed his way to the car.

"What's up?" he asked; for he was the company's surgeon.

"Well, there's wan dead, wan dying, and we're all more or less kilt," said Shea, pushing the mob back to give the doctor room.

Lifting Lucien's head, the doctor held a small bottle under his nose, and the wounded man came out. Strong, and the reporter would say "willing hands," now lifted the car bodily from the track and put it down on the platform near the baggage-room.

When the doctor had revived the French-Canadian and stopped the flow of blood, he took the boss in hand. Opening the man's clothes, he searched for the wound, but found none.

They literally stripped Kelly to the waist; but there was not a scratch to be found upon his body. When the doctor declared it to be his opinion that Kelly was not hurt at all, but had merely fainted, Kelly was indignant.

Of course the whole accident (Lucien being seriously hurt) had to be investigated, and this was the finding of the experts:—

A tin torpedo left on the rail by a flagman was exploded by the wheel of the hand-car. A piece of tin flew up, caught Lucien in the neck, making a nasty wound. Lucien was thrown from the car, when it jumped the track, so violently as to render him unconscious. Kelly and Burke and Shea, picking themselves up, one after the other, each fainted dead away at the sight of so much blood.

Lucien revived first, took in the situation, loaded the limp bodies, and pulled for home, and that is the true story of the awful wreck on the Père Marquette.

THE STORY OF AN ENGLISHMAN

A young Englishman stood watching a freight train pulling out of a new town, over a new track. A pinch-bar, left carelessly by a section gang, caught in the cylinder-cock rigging and tore it off.

Swearing softly, the driver climbed down and began the nasty work of disconnecting the disabled machinery. He was not a machinist. Not all engine-drivers can put a locomotive together. In fact the best runners are just runners. The Englishman stood by and, when he saw the man fumble his wrench, offered a hand. The driver, with some hesitation, gave him the tools, and in a few minutes the crippled rigging was taken down, nuts replaced, and the rigging passed by the Englishman to the fireman, who threw it up on the rear of the tank.

"Are you a mechanic?" asked the driver.

"Yes, sir," said the Englishman, standing at least a foot above the engineer. "There's a job for me up the road, if I can get there."

"And you're out of tallow?"

The Englishman was not quite sure; but he guessed "tallow" was United States for "money," and said he was short.

"All right," said the engine-driver; "climb on."

The fireman was a Dutchman named Martin, and he made the Englishman comfortable; but the Englishman wanted to work. He wanted to help fire the engine, and Martin showed him how to do it, taking her himself on the hills. When they pulled into the town of E., the Englishman went over to the round-house and the foreman asked him if he had ever "railroaded." He said No, but he was a machinist. "Well, I don't want you," said the foreman, and the Englishman went across to the little eating-stand where the trainmen were having dinner. Martin moved over and made room for the stranger between himself and his engineer.

"What luck?" asked the latter.

"Hard luck," was the answer, and without more talk the men hurried on through the meal.

They had to eat dinner and do an hour's switching in twenty minutes. That is an easy trick when nobody is looking. You arrive, eat dinner, then register in. That is the first the despatcher hears of you at E. You switch twenty minutes and register out. That is the last the despatcher hears of you at E. You switch another twenty minutes and go. That is called stealing time; and may the Manager have mercy on you if you're caught at it, for you've got to make up that last twenty minutes before you hit the next station.

As the engineer dropped a little oil here and there for another dash, the Englishman came up to the engine. He could not bring himself to ask the driver for another ride, and he didn't need to.

"You don't get de jobs?" asked Martin.

"No."

"Vell, dat's all right; you run his railroad some day."

"I don't like the agent here," said the driver; "but if you were up at the other end of the yard, over on the left-hand side, he couldn't see you, and I couldn't see you for the steam from that broken cylinder-cock."

Now they say an Englishman is slow to catch on, but this one was not; and as the engine rattled over the last switch, he climbed into the cab in a cloud of steam. Martin made him welcome again, pointing to a seat on the waste-box. The dead-head took off his coat, folded it carefully, laid it on the box, and reached for the shovel. "Not yet," said Martin, "dare is holes already in de fire; I must get dose yello smoke from de shtack off."

The dead-head leaned from the window, watching the stack burn clear, then Martin gave him the shovel. Half-way up a long, hard hill the pointer on the steam-gauge began to go back. The driver glanced over at Martin, and Martin took the shovel. The dead-head climbed up on the tank and shovelled the coal down into the pit, that was now nearly empty. In a little while they pulled into the town of M.C., Iowa, at the crossing of the Chicago, Milwaukee, and St. Paul. Here the Englishman had to change cars. His destination was on the cross-road, still one hundred and eighteen miles away. The engine-driver took the joint agent to one side, the agent wrote on a small piece of paper, folded it carefully, and gave it to the Englishman. "This may help you," said he; "be quick—they're just pulling out—run!"

Panting, the Englishman threw himself into a way-car that was already making ten miles an hour. The train official unfolded the paper, read it, looked the Englishman over, and said, "All right."

It was nearly night when the train arrived at W., and the dead-head followed the train crew into an unpainted pine hotel, where all hands fell eagerly to work. A man stood behind a little high desk at the door taking money; but when the Englishman offered to pay he said, "Yours is paid fer."

"Not mine; nobody knows me here."

"Then, 'f the devil don't know you better than I do you're lost, young man," said the landlord. "But some one p'inted to you and said, 'I pay fer him.' It ain't a thing to make a noise about. It don't make no difference to me whether it's Tom or Jerry that pays, so long as everybody represents."

"Well, this is a funny country," mused the Englishman, as he strolled over to the shop. Now when he heard the voice of the foreman, with its musical burr, which stamped the man as a Briton from the Highlands, his heart grew glad. The Scotchman listened to the stranger's story without any sign of emotion or even interest; and when he learned that the man had "never railroaded," but had been all his life in the British Government service, he said he could do nothing for him, and walked away.

The young man sat and thought it over, and concluded he would see the master-mechanic. On the following morning he found that official at his desk and told his story. He had just arrived from England with a wife and three children and a few dollars. "That's all right," said the master-mechanic; "I'll give you a job on Monday morning."

This was Saturday, and during the day the first foreman with whom the Englishman had talked wired that if he would return to E. he could find work. The young man showed this wire to the master-mechanic. "I should like to work for you," said he; "you have been very kind to give me employment after the foreman had refused, but my family is near this place. They are two hundred miles or more from here."

"I understand," said the kind-hearted official, "and you'd better go back to E."

The Englishman rubbed his chin and looked out of the window. The train standing at the station and about to pull out would carry him back to the junction, but he made no effort to catch it, and the master-mechanic, seeing this, caught the drift of the young man's mind. "Have you transportation?" he asked. The stranger, smiling, shook his head. Turning to his desk, the master-mechanic wrote a pass to the junction and a telegram requesting transportation over the Iowa Central from the junction to the town of E.

That Sunday the young man told his young wife that the new country was "all right." Everybody trusted everybody else. An official would give a stranger free transportation; a station agent could give you a pass, and even an engine-driver could carry a man without asking permission.

He didn't know that all these men save the master-mechanic had violated the rules of the road and endangered their own positions and the chance of promotion by helping him; but he felt he was among good, kind people, and thanked them just the same.

On Monday morning he went to work in the little shop. In a little while he was one of the trustworthy men employed in the place. "How do you square a locomotive?" he asked the foreman. "Here," said the foreman; "from this point to that."

That was all the Englishman asked. He stretched a line between the given points and went to work.

Two years from this the town of M. offered to donate to the railroad company $47,000 if the new machine shop could be located there, steam up and machinery running, on the first day of January of the following year.

The general master-mechanic entrusted the work of putting in the machinery, after the walls had been built and the place roofed over, to the division master-mechanic, who looked to the local foreman to finish the job in time to win the subsidy.

The best months of the year went by before work was begun. Frost came, and the few men tinkering about were chilled by the autumn winds that were wailing through the shutterless doors and glassless windows. Finally the foreman sent the Englishman to M. to help put up the machinery. He was a new man, and therefore was expected to take signals from the oldest man on the job,—a sort of straw-boss.

The bridge boss—the local head of the wood-workers—found the Englishman gazing about, and the two men talked together. There was no foreman there, but the Englishman thought he ought to work anyway; so he and the wood boss stretched a line for a line-shaft, and while the carpenter's gang put up braces and brackets the Englishman coupled the shaft together, and in a few days it was ready to go up. As the young man worked and whistled away one morning, the boss carpenter came in with a military-looking gentleman, who seemed to own the place. "Where did you come from?" asked the new-comer of the machinist.

"From England, sir."

"Well, anybody could tell that. Where did you come from when you came here?"

"From E."

"Well, sir, can you finish this job and have steam up here on the first of January?"

The Englishman blushed, for he was embarrassed, and glanced at the wood boss. Then, sweeping the almost empty shop with his eye, he said something about a foreman who was in charge of the work. "Damn the foreman," said the stranger; "I'm talking to you."

The young man blushed again, and said he could work twelve or fourteen hours a day for a time if it were necessary, but he didn't like to make any rash promises about the general result.

"Now look here," said the well-dressed man, "I want you to take charge of this job and finish it; employ as many men as you can handle, and blow a whistle here on New Year's morning—do you understand?"

The Englishman thought he did, but he could hardly believe it. He glanced at the wood boss, and the wood boss nodded his head.

"I shall do my best," said the Englishman, taking courage, "but I should like to know who gives these orders."

"I'm the General Manager," said the man; "now get a move on you," and he turned and walked out.

It is not to be supposed that the General Manager saw anything remarkable about the young man, save that he was six feet and had a good face. The fact is, the wood foreman had boomed the Englishman's stock before the Manager saw him.

The path of the Englishman was not strewn with flowers for the next few months. Any number of men who had been on the road when he was in the English navy-yards felt that they ought to have had this little promotion. The local foremen along the line saw in the young Englishman the future foreman of the new shops, and no man went out of his way to help the stranger. But in spite of all obstacles, the shop grew from day to day, from week to week; so that as the old year drew to a close the machinery was getting into place. The young foreman, while a hard worker, was always pleasant in his intercourse with the employees, and in a little while he had hosts of friends. There is always a lot of extra work at the end of a big job, and now when Christmas came there was still much to do. The men worked night and day. The boiler that was to come from Chicago had been expected for some time. Everything was in readiness, and it could be set up in a day; but it did not come. Tracer-letters that had gone after it were followed by telegrams; finally it was located in a wreck out in a cornfield in Illinois on the last day of the year.

A great many of the officials were away, and the service was generally demoralized during the holidays, so that the appropriation for which the Englishman was working at M. had for the moment been forgotten; the shops were completed, the machinery was in, but there was no boiler to boil water to make steam.

That night, when the people of M. were watching the old year out and the new year in, the young Englishman with a force of men was wrecking the pump-house down by the station. The little upright boiler was torn out and placed in the machine shops, and with it a little engine was driven that turned the long line-shaft.

At dawn they ran a long pipe through the roof, screwed a locomotive whistle on the top of it, and at six o'clock on New Year's morning the new whistle on the new shops at M. in Iowa, blew in the new year. Incidentally, it blew the town in for $47,000.

This would be a good place to end this story, but the temptation is great to tell the rest.

When the shops were opened, the young Englishman was foreman. This was only about twenty-five years ago. In a little while they promoted him.

In 1887 he went to the Wisconsin Central. In 1890 he was made Superintendent of machinery of the Santa Fé route,—one of the longest roads on earth. It begins at Chicago, strong like a man's wrist, with a finger each on Sacramento, San Francisco, San Diego, and El Paso, and a thumb touching the Gulf at Galveston.

The mileage of the system, at that time, was equal to one-half that of Great Britain; and upon the companies' payrolls were ten thousand more men than were then in the army of the United States. Fifteen hundred men and boys walk into the main shops at Topeka every morning. They work four hours, eat luncheon, listen to a lecture or short sermon in the meeting-place above the shops, work another four hours, and walk out three thousand dollars better off than they would have been if they had not worked.

These shops make a little city of themselves. There is a perfect water system, fire-brigade with fire stations where the firemen sleep, police, and a dog-catcher.

Here they build anything of wood, iron, brass, or steel that the company needs, from a ninety-ton locomotive to a single-barrelled mouse-trap, all under the eye of the Englishman who came to America with a good wife and three babies, a good head and two hands. This man's name is John Player. He is the inventor of the Player truck, the Player hand-car, the Player frog, and many other useful appliances.

This simple story of an unpretentious man came out in broken sections as the special sped along the smooth track, while the General Manager talked with the resident director and the General Superintendent talked with his assistant, who, not long ago, was the conductor of a work-train upon which the G.S. was employed as brakeman. I was two days stealing this story, between the blushes of the mechanical Superintendent.

He related, also, that a man wearing high-cut trousers and milk on his boot had entered his office when he had got to his first position as master-mechanic and held out a hand, smiling, "Vell, you don't know me yet, ain't it? I'm Martin the fireman; I quit ranchin' already, an' I want a jobs."

Martin got a job at once. He got killed, also, in a little while; but that is part of the business on a new road.

Near the shops at Topeka stands the railroad Young Men's Christian Association building. They were enlarging it when I was there. There are no "saloons" in Kansas, so Player and his company help the men to provide other amusements.

ON THE LIMITED

One Sabbath evening, not long ago, I went down to the depot in an Ontario town to take the International Limited for Montreal. She was on the blackboard five minutes in disgrace. "Huh!" grunted a commercial traveller. It was Sunday in the aforesaid Ontario town, and would be Sunday in Toronto, toward which he was travelling. Even if we were on time we should not arrive until 9.30—too late for church, too early to go to bed, and the saloons all closed and barred. And yet this restless traveller fretted and grieved because we promised to get into Toronto five minutes late. Alas for the calculation of the train despatchers, she was seven minutes overdue when she swept in and stood for us to mount. The get-away was good, but at the eastern yard limits we lost again. The people from the Pullmans piled into the café car and overflowed into the library and parlor cars. The restless traveller snapped his watch again, caught the sleeve of a passing trainman, and asked "'S matter?" and the conductor answered, "Waiting for No. 5." Five minutes passed and not a wheel turned; six, eight, ten minutes, and no sound of the coming west-bound express. Up ahead we could hear the flutter and flap of the blow-off; for the black flier was as restless as the fat drummer who was snapping his watch, grunting "Huh," and washing suppressed profanity down with café noir.

Eighteen minutes and No. 5 passed. When the great black steed of steam got them swinging again we were twenty-five minutes to the bad. And how that driver did hit the curves! The impatient traveller snapped his watch again and said, refusing to be comforted, "She'll never make it."

Mayhap the fat and fretful drummer managed to communicate with the engine-driver, or maybe the latter was unhappily married or had an insurance policy; and it is also possible that he is just the devil to drive. Anyway, he whipped that fine train of Pullmans, café, and parlor cars through those peaceful, lamplighted, Sabbath-keeping Ontario towns as though the whole show had cost not more than seven dollars, and his own life less.

On a long lounge in the library car a well-nourished lawyer lay sleeping in a way that I had not dreamed a political lawyer could sleep. One gamey M.P.—double P, I was told—had been robbing this same lawyer of a good deal of rest recently, and he was trying at a mile a minute to catch up with his sleep. I could feel the sleeper slam her flanges against the ball of the rail as we rounded the perfectly pitched curves, and the little semi-quaver that tells the trained traveller that the man up ahead is moving the mile-posts, at least one every minute. At the first stop, twenty-five miles out, the fat drummer snapped his watch again, but he did not say, "Huh." We had made up five minutes.

A few passengers swung down here, and a few others swung up; and off we dashed, drilling the darkness. I looked in on the lawyer again, for I would have speech with him; but he was still sleeping the sleep of the virtuous, with the electric light full on his upturned baby face, that reminds me constantly of the late Tom Reed.

A woman I know was putting one of her babies to bed in lower 2, when we wiggled through a reverse curve that was like shooting White Horse Rapids in a Peterboro. The child intended for lower 2 went over into 4. "Never mind," said its mother, "we have enough to go around;" and so she left that one in 4 and put the next one in 2, and so on.

At the next stop where you "Y" and back into the town, the people, impatient, were lined up, ready to board the Limited. When we swung over the switches again, we were only ten minutes late.

As often as the daring driver eased off for a down grade I could hear the hiss of steam through the safety-valve above the back of the black flier, and I could feel the flanges against the ball of the rail, and the little tell-tale semi-quaver of the car.

By now the babies were all abed; and from bunk to bunk she tucked them in, kissed them good-night, and then cuddled down beside the last one, a fair-haired girl who seemed to have caught and kept, in her hair and in her eyes, the sunshine of the three short summers through which she had passed.

Once more I went and stood by the lounge where the lawyer lay, but I had not the nerve to wake him.

The silver moon rose and lit the ripples on the lake that lay below my window as the last of the diners came from the café car. Along the shore of the sleeping lake our engine swept like a great, black, wingless bird of night. Presently I felt the frogs of South Parkdale; and when, from her hot throat she called "Toronto," the fat and fretful traveller opened his great gold watch. He did not snap it now, but looked into its open face and almost smiled; for we were touching Toronto on the tick of time.

I stepped from the car, for I was interested in the fat drummer. I wanted to see him meet her, and hold her hand, and tell her what a really, truly, good husband he had been, and how he had hurried home. As he came down the short stair a friend faced him and said "Good-night," where we say "Good-evening." "Hello, Bill," said the fat drummer. They shook hands languidly. The fat man yawned and asked, "Anything doing?" "Not the littlest," said Bill. "Then," said Jim (the fat man), "let us go up to the King Edward, sit down, and have a good, quiet smoke."

THE CONQUEST OF ALASKA

Immediately under the man with the money, who lived in London, there was the President in Chicago; then came the chief engineer in Seattle, the locating engineer in Skagway, the contractor in the grading camp, and Hugh Foy, the "boss" of the builders. Yet in spite of all this overhanging stratification, Foy was a big man. To be sure, none of these men had happened to get their positions by mere chance. They were men of character and fortitude, capable of great sacrifice.

Mr. Close, in London, knew that his partner, Mr. Graves, in Chicago, would be a good man at the head of so cold and hopeless an enterprise as a Klondike Railway; and Mr. Graves knew that Erastus Corning Hawkins, who had put through some of the biggest engineering schemes in the West, was the man to build the road. The latter selected, as locating engineer, John Hislop, the hero, one of the few survivors of that wild and daring expedition that undertook, some twenty years ago, to survey a route for a railroad whose trains were to traverse the Grand Cañon of Colorado, where, save for the song of the cataract, there is only shade and silence and perpetual starlight. Heney, a wiry, compact, plucky Canadian contractor, made oral agreement with the chief engineer and, with Hugh Foy as his superintendent of construction, began to grade what they called the White Pass and Yukon Railway. Beginning where the bone-washing Skagway tells her troubles to the tide-waters at the elbow of that beautiful arm of the Pacific Ocean called Lynn Canal, they graded out through the scattered settlement where a city stands to-day, cut through a dense forest of spruce, and began to climb the hill.

When the news of ground-breaking had gone out to Seattle and Chicago, and thence to London, conservative capitalists, who had suspected Close Brothers and Company and all their associates in this wild scheme of temporary insanity, concluded that the sore affliction had come to stay. But the dauntless builders on the busy field where the grading camp was in action kept grubbing and grading, climbing and staking, blasting and building, undiscouraged and undismayed. Under the eaves of a dripping glacier, Hawkins, Hislop, and Heney crept; and, as they measured off the miles and fixed the grade by blue chalk-marks where stakes could not be driven, Foy followed with his army of blasters and builders. When the pathfinders came to a deep side cañon, they tumbled down, clambered up on the opposite side, found their bearings, and began again. At one place the main wall was so steep that the engineer was compelled to climb to the top, let a man down by a rope, so that he could mark the face of the cliff for the blasters, and then haul him up again.

It was springtime when they began, and through the long days of that short summer the engineers explored and mapped and located; and ever, close behind them, they could hear the steady roar of Foy's fireworks as the skilled blasters burst big boulders or shattered the shoulders of great crags that blocked the trail of the iron horse. Ever and anon, when the climbers and builders peered down into the ragged cañon, they saw a long line of pack-animals, bipeds and quadrupeds,—some hoofed and some horned, some bleeding, some blind,—stumbling and staggering, fainting and falling, the fittest fighting for the trail and gaining the summit, whence the clear, green waters of the mighty Yukon would carry them down to Dawson,— the Mecca of all these gold-mad men. As often as the road-makers glanced at the pack-trains, they saw hundreds of thousands of dollars' worth of traffic going past or waiting transportation at Skagway, and each strained every nerve to complete the work while the sun shone.

By midsummer they began to appreciate the fact that this was to be a hard job. When the flowers faded on the southern slopes, they were not more than half-way up the hill. Each day the sun swung lower across the canals, all the to-morrows were shorter than the yesterdays, and there was not a man among them with a shade of sentiment, or a sense of the beautiful, but sighed when the flowers died. Yes, they had learned to love this maiden, Summer, that had tripped up from the south, smiled on them, sung for a season, sighed, smiled once more, and then danced down the Lynn again.

"I'll come back," she seemed to say, peeping over the shoulder of a glacier that stood at the stage entrance; "I'll come back, but ere I come again there'll be strange scenes and sounds on this rude stage so new to you. First, you will have a short season of melodrama by a melancholy chap called Autumn, gloriously garbed in green and gold, with splashes and dashes of lavender and lace, but sad, sweetly sad, and sighing always, for life is such a little while."

With a sadder smile, she kissed her rosy fingers and was gone,—gone with her gorgeous garments, her ferns and flowers, her low, soft sighs and sunny skies, and there was not a man that was a man but missed her when she was gone.

The autumn scene, though sombre and sad, was far from depressing, but they all felt the change. John Hislop seemed to feel it more than all the rest; for besides being deeply religious, he was deeply in love. His nearest and dearest friend, Heney—happy, hilarious Heney—knew, and he swore softly whenever a steamer landed without a message from Minneapolis,—the long-looked-for letter that would make Hislop better or worse. It came at length, and Hislop was happy. With his horse, his dog, and a sandwich,—but never a gun,—he would make long excursions down toward Lake Linderman, to Bennett, or over Atlin way. When the country became too rough for the horse, he would be left picketed near a stream with a faithful dog to look after him while the pathfinder climbed up among the eagles.

In the meantime Foy kept pounding away. Occasionally a soiled pedestrian would slide down the slope, tell a wild tale of rich strikes, and a hundred men would quit work and head for the highlands. Foy would storm and swear and coax by turns, but to no purpose; for they were like so many steers, and as easily stampeded. When the Atlin boom struck the camp, Foy lost five hundred men in as many minutes. Scores of graders dropped their tools and started off on a trot. The prospector who had told the fable had thrown his thumb over his shoulder to indicate the general direction. Nobody had thought to ask how far. Many forgot to let go; and Heney's picks and shovels, worth over a dollar apiece, went away with the stampeders. As the wild mob swept on, the tethered blasters cut the cables that guyed them to the hills, and each loped away with a piece of rope around one ankle.

Panting, they passed over the range, these gold-crazed Coxeys, without a bun or a blanket, a crust or a crumb, many without a cent or even a sweat-mark where a cent had slept in their soiled overalls.

When Foy had exhausted the English, Irish, and Alaskan languages in wishing the men luck in various degrees, he rounded up the remnant of his army and began again. In a day or two the stampeders began to limp back hungry and weary, and every one who brought a pick or a shovel was re-employed. But hundreds kept on toward Lake Bennett, and thence by water up Windy Arm to the Atlin country, and many of them have not yet returned to claim their time-checks.

The autumn waned. The happy wives of young engineers, who had been tented along the line during the summer, watched the wildflowers fade with a feeling of loneliness and deep longing for their stout-hearted, strong-limbed husbands, who were away up in the cloud-veiled hills; and they longed, too, for other loved ones in the lowlands of their childhood. Foy's blasters and builders buttoned their coats and buckled down to keep warm. Below, they could hear loud peals of profanity as the trailers, packers, and pilgrims pounded their dumb slaves over the trail. Above, the wind cried and moaned among the crags, constantly reminding them that winter was near at hand. The nights were longer than the days. The working day was cut from ten to eight hours, but the pay of the men had been raised from thirty to thirty-five cents an hour.

One day a black cloud curtained the cañon, and the workmen looked up from their picks and drills to find that it was November and night. The whole theatre, stage and all, had grown suddenly dark; but they knew, by the strange, weird noise in the wings, that the great tragedy of winter was on. Hislop's horse and dog went down the trail. Hawkins and Hislop and Heney walked up and down among the men, as commanding officers show themselves on the eve of battle. Foy chaffed the laborers and gave them more rope; but no amount of levity could prevail against the universal feeling of dread that seemed to settle upon the whole army. This weird Alaska, so wild and grand, so cool and sweet and sunny in summer, so strangely sad in autumn,—this many-mooded, little known Alaska that seemed doomed ever to be misunderstood, either over-lauded or lied about,—what would she do to them? How cruel, how cold, how weird, how wickedly wild her winters must be! Most men are brave, and an army of brave men will breast great peril when God's lamp lights the field; but the stoutest heart dreads the darkness. These men were sore afraid, all of them; and yet no one was willing to be the first to fall out, so they stood their ground. They worked with a will born of desperation.

The wind moaned hoarsely. The temperature dropped to thirty-five degrees below zero, but the men, in sheltered places, kept pounding. Sometimes they would work all day cleaning the snow from the grade made the day before, and the next day it would probably be drifted full again. At times the task seemed hopeless; but Heney had promised to build to the summit of White Pass without a stop, and Foy had given Heney his hand across a table at the Fifth Avenue Hotel in Skagway.

At times the wind blew so frightfully that the men had to hold hands; but they kept pegging away between blasts, and in a little while were ready to begin bridging the gulches and deep side-cañons. One day—or one night, rather, for there were no days then—a camp cook, crazed by the cold and the endless night, wandered off to die. Hislop and Heney found him, but he refused to be comforted. He wanted to quit, but Heney said he could not be spared. He begged to be left alone to sleep in the warm, soft snow, but Heney brought him back to consciousness and to camp.

A premature blast blew a man into eternity. The wind moaned still more drearily. The snow drifted deeper and deeper, and one day they found that, for days and days, they had been blasting ice and snow when they thought they were drilling the rock. Heney and Foy faced each other in the dim light of a tent lamp that night. "Must we give up?" asked the contractor.

"No," said Foy, slowly, speaking in a whisper; "we'll build on snow, for it's hard and safe; and in the spring we'll ease it down and make a road-bed."

They did so. They built and bedded the cross-ties on the snow, ballasted with snow, and ran over that track until spring without an accident.

They were making mileage slowly, but the awful strain was telling on the men and on the bank account. The president of the company was almost constantly travelling between Washington and Ottawa, pausing now and again to reach over to London for another bag of gold, for they were melting it up there in the arctic night—literally burning it up, were these dynamiters of Foy's.

To conceive this great project, to put it into shape, present it in London, secure the funds and the necessary concessions from two governments, survey and build, and have a locomotive running in Alaska a year from the first whoop of the happy Klondiker, had been a mighty achievement; but it was what Heney would call "dead easy" compared with the work that confronted the President at this time. On July 20, 1897, the first pick was driven into the ground at White Pass; just a year later the pioneer locomotive was run over the road. More than once had the financial backers allowed their faith in the enterprise and in the future of the country beyond to slip away; but the President of the company had always succeeded in building it up again, for they had never lost faith in him, or in his ability to see things that were to most men invisible. In summer, when the weekly reports showed a mile or more or less of track laid, it was not so hard; but when days were spent in placing a single bent in a bridge, and weeks were consumed on a switch back in a pinched-out cañon, it was hard to persuade sane men that business sense demanded that they pile on more fuel. But they did it; and, as the work went on, it became apparent to those interested in such undertakings that all the heroes of the White Pass were not in the hills.

In addition to the elements, ever at war with the builders, they had other worries that winter. Hawkins had a fire that burned all the company's offices and all his maps and notes and records of surveys. Foy had a strike, incited largely by jealous packers and freighters; and there was hand-to-hand fighting between the strikers and their abettors and the real builders, who sympathized with the company.

Brydone-Jack, a fine young fellow, who had been sent out as consulting engineer to look after the interests of the shareholders, clapped his hands to his forehead and fell, face down, in the snow. His comrades carried him to his tent. He had been silent, had suffered, perhaps for a day or two, but had said nothing. The next night he passed away. His wife was waiting at Vancouver until he could finish his work in Alaska and go home to her.

With sad and heavy hearts Hawkins and Hislop and Heney climbed back to where Foy and his men were keeping up the fight. Like so many big lightning-bugs they seemed, with their dim white lamps rattling around in the storm. It was nearly all night then. God and his sunlight seemed to have forsaken Alaska. Once every twenty-four hours a little ball of fire, red, round, and remote, swung across the cañon, dimly lighted their lunch-tables, and then disappeared behind the great glacier that guards the gateway to the Klondike.

As the road neared the summit, Heney observed that Foy was growing nervous, and that he coughed a great deal. He watched the old fellow, and found that he was not eating well, and that he slept very little. Heney asked Foy to rest, but the latter shook his head. Hawkins and Hislop and Heney talked the matter over in Hislop's tent, called Foy in, and demanded that he go down and out. Foy was coughing constantly, but he choked it back long enough to tell the three men what he thought of them. He had worked hard and faithfully to complete the job, and now that only one level mile remained to be railed, would they send the old man down the hill? "I will not budge," said Foy, facing his friends; "an' when you gentlemen ar-re silibratin' th' vict'ry at the top o' the hill ahn Chuesday nixt, Hugh Foy'll be wood ye. Do you moind that, now?"

Foy steadied himself by a tent-pole and coughed violently. His eyes were glassy, and his face flushed with the purplish flush that fever gives.

"Enough of this!" said the chief engineer, trying to look severe. "Take this message, sign it, and send it at once."

Foy caught the bit of white clip and read:—

"Captain O'Brien,

Skagway.

"Save a berth for me on the 'Rosalie.'"

They thought, as they watched him, that the old road-maker was about to crush the paper in his rough right hand; but suddenly his face brightened, he reached for a pencil, saying, "I'll do it," and when he had added "next trip" to the message, he signed it, folded it, and took it over to the operator.

So it happened that, when the last spike was driven at the summit, on February 20, 1899, the old foreman, who had driven the first, drove the last, and it was his last spike as well. Doctor Whiting guessed it was pneumonia.

When the road had been completed to Lake Bennett, the owners came over to see it; and when they saw what had been done, despite the prediction that Dawson was dead and that the Cape Nome boom would equal that of the Klondike, they authorized the construction of another hundred miles of road which would connect with the Yukon below the dreaded White Horse Rapids. Jack and Foy and Hislop are gone; and when John Hislop passed away, the West lost one of the most modest and unpretentious, yet one of the best and bravest, one of the purest minded men that ever saw the sun go down behind a snowy range.

NUMBER THREE

One winter night, as the west-bound express was pulling out of Omaha, a drunken man climbed aboard. The young Superintendent, who stood on the rear platform, caught the man by the collar and hauled him up the steps.

The train, from the tank to the tail-lights, was crammed full of passenger-people going home or away to spend Christmas. Over in front the express and baggage cars were piled full of baggage, bundles, boxes, trinkets, and toys, each intended to make some heart happier on the morrow, for it was Christmas Eve. It was to see that these passengers and their precious freight, already a day late, got through that the Superintendent was leaving his own fireside to go over the road.

The snow came swirling across the plain, cold and wet, pasting the window and blurring the headlight on the black locomotive that was climbing laboriously over the kinks and curves of a new track. Here and there, in sheltered wimples, bands of buffalo were bunched to shield them from the storm. Now and then an antelope left the rail or a lone coyote crouched in the shadow of a telegraph-pole as the dim headlight swept the right of way. At each stop the Superintendent would jump down, look about, and swing onto the rear car as the train pulled out again. At one time he found that his seat had been taken, also his overcoat, which had been left hanging over the back. The thief was discovered on the blind baggage and turned over to the "city marshal" at the next stop.

Upon entering the train again, the Superintendent went forward to find a seat in the express car. It was near midnight now. They were coming into a settlement and passing through prosperous new towns that were building up near the end of the division. Near the door the messenger had set a little green Christmas tree, and grouped about it were a red sled, a doll-carriage, some toys, and a few parcels. If the blond doll in the little toy carriage toppled over, the messenger would set it up again; and when passing freight out he was careful not to knock a twig from the tree. So intent was he upon the task of taking care of this particular shipment that he had forgotten the Superintendent, and started and almost stared at him when he shouted the observation that the messenger was a little late with his tree.

"'Tain't mine," he said sadly, shaking his head. "B'longs to the fellow 't swiped your coat."

"No!" exclaimed the Superintendent, as he went over to look at the toys.

"If he'd only asked me," said the messenger, more to himself than to the Superintendent, "he could 'a' had mine and welcome."

"Do you know the man?"

"Oh, yes—he lives next door to me, and I'll have to face his wife and lie to her, and then face my own; but I can't lie to her. I'll tell her the truth and get roasted for letting Downs get away. I'll go to sleep by the sound of her sobs and wake to find her crying in her coffee—that's the kind of a Christmas I'll have. When he's drunk he's disgusting, of course; but when he's sober he's sorry. And Charley Downs is honest."

"Honest!" shouted the Superintendent.

"Yes, I know he took your coat, but that wasn't Charley Downs; it was the tarantula-juice he'd been imbibing in Omaha. Left alone he's as honest as I am; and here's a run that would trip up a missionary. For instance, leaving Loneville the other night, a man came running alongside the car and threw in a bundle of bills that looked like a bale of hay. Not a scrap of paper or pencil-mark, just a wad o' winnings with a wang around the middle. 'A Christmas gift for my wife,' he yelled. 'How much?' I shouted. 'Oh, I dunno—whole lot, but it's tied good'; and then a cloud of steam from the cylinder-cocks came between us, and I haven't seen him since.

"For the past six months Downs has tried hard to be decent, and has succeeded some; and this was to be the supreme test. For six months his wife has been saving up to send him to Omaha to buy things for Christmas. If he could do that, she argued, and come back sober, he'd be stronger to begin the New Year. Of course they looked to me to keep him on the rail, and I did. I shadowed him from shop to shop until he bought all the toys and some little trinkets for his wife. Always I found he had paid and ordered the things to be sent to the express office marked to me.

"Well, finally I followed him to a clothing store, where, according to a promise made to his wife, he bought an overcoat, the first he had felt on his back for years. This he put on, of course, for it is cold in Omaha to-day; and I left him and slipped away to grab a few hours' sleep.

"When I woke I went out to look for him, but could not find him, though I tried hard, and came to my car without supper. I found his coat, however, hung up in a saloon, and redeemed it, hoping still to find Charley before train time. I watched for him until we were signalled out, and then went back and looked through the train, but failed to find him.

"Of course I am sorry for Charley," the messenger went on after a pause, "but more so for the poor little woman. She's worked and worked, and saved and saved, and hoped and dreamed, until she actually believed he'd been cured and that the sun would shine in her life again. Why, the neighbors have been talking across the back fence about how well Mrs. Downs was looking. My wife declared she heard her laugh the other day clear over to our house. Half the town knew about her dream. The women folks have been carrying work to her and then going over and helping her do it as a sort of surprise party. And now it's all off. To-morrow will be Christmas; and he'll be in jail, his wife in despair, and I in disgrace. Charley Downs a thief—in jail! It'll just break her heart!"

The whistle proclaimed a stop, and the Superintendent swung out with a lump in his throat. This was an important station, and the last one before Loneville. Without looking to the right or left, the Superintendent walked straight to the telegraph office and sent the following message to the agent at the place where Downs had been ditched:—

"Turn that fellow loose and send him to Loneville on three—all a joke.

"W.C.V., Superintendent."

In a little while the train was rattling over the road again; and when the engine screamed for Loneville, the Superintendent stood up and looked at the messenger.

"What'll I tell her?" the latter asked.

"Well, he got left at Cactus sure enough, didn't he? If that doesn't satisfy her, tell her that he may get over on No. 3."

When the messenger had turned his freight over to the driver of the Fargo wagon, he gathered up the Christmas tree and the toys and trudged homeward, looking like Santa Claus, so completely hidden was he by the tree and the trinkets. As he neared the Downs' home, the door swung open, the lamplight shone out upon him, and he saw two women smiling from the open door. It took but one glance at the messenger's face to show them that something was wrong, and the smiles faded. Mrs. Downs received the shock without a murmur, leaning on her friend and leaving the marks of her fingers on her friend's arm.

The messenger put the toys down suddenly, silently; and feeling that the unhappy woman would be better alone, the neighbors departed, leaving her seated by the window, peering into the night, the lamp turned very low.

The little clock on the shelf above the stove ticked off the seconds, measured the minutes, and marked the melancholy hours. The storm ceased, the stars came out and showed the quiet town asleep beneath its robe of white. The clock was now striking four, and she had scarcely stirred. She was thinking of the watchers of Bethlehem, when suddenly a great light shone on the eastern horizon. At last the freight was coming. She had scarcely noticed the messenger's suggestion that Charley might come in on three. Now she waited, with just the faintest ray of hope; and after a long while the deep voice of the locomotive came to her, the long black train crept past and stopped. Now her heart beat wildly. Somebody was coming up the road. A moment later she recognized her erring husband, dressed exactly as he had been when he left home, his short coat buttoned close up under his chin. When she saw him approaching slowly but steadily, she knew he was sober and doubtless cold. She was about to fling the door open to admit him when he stopped and stood still. She watched him. He seemed to be wringing his hands. An awful thought chilled her,—the thought that the cold and exposure had unbalanced his mind. Suddenly he knelt in the snow and turned his sad face up to the quiet sky. He was praying, and with a sudden impulse she fell upon her knees and they prayed together with only the window-glass between them.

When the prodigal got to his feet, the door stood open and his wife was waiting to receive him. At sight of her, dressed as she had been when he left her, a sudden flame of guilt and shame burned through him; but it served only to clear his brain and strengthen his will-power, which all his life had been so weak, and lately made weaker for want of exercise. He walked almost hurriedly to the chair she set for him near the stove, and sank into it with the weary air of one who has been long in bed. She felt of his hands and they were not cold. She touched his face and found it warm. She pushed the dark hair from his pale forehead and kissed it. She knelt and prayed again, her head upon his knee. He bowed above her while she prayed, and stroked her hair. She felt his tears falling upon her head. She stood up, and when he lifted his face to hers, looked into his wide weeping eyes,—aye, into his very soul. She liked to see the tears and the look of agony on his face, for she knew by these signs how he suffered, and she knew why.

When he had grown calm she brought a cup of coffee to him. He drank it, and then she led him to the little dining-room, where a midnight supper had been set for four, but, because of his absence, had not been touched. He saw the tree and the toys that the messenger had left, and spoke for the first time. "Oh, wife dear, have they all come? Are they all here? The toys and all?" and then, seeing the overcoat that the messenger had left on a chair near by, and which his wife had not yet seen, he cried excitedly, "Take that away—it isn't mine!"

"Why, yes, dear," said his wife, "it must be yours."

"No, no," he said; "I bought a coat like that, but I sold it. I drank a lot and only climbed on the train as it was pulling out of Omaha. In the warm car I fell asleep and dreamed the sweetest dream I ever knew. I had come home sober with all the things, you had kissed me, we had a great dinner here, and there stood the Christmas tree, the children were here, the messenger and his wife, and their children. We were all so happy! I saw the shadow fade from your face, saw you smile and heard you laugh; saw the old love-light in your eyes and the rose coming into your cheek. And then—'Oh, bitterness of things too sweet!'—I woke to find my own old trembling self again. It was all a dream. Looking across the aisle, I saw that coat on the back of an empty seat. I knew it was not mine, for I had sold mine for two miserable dollars. I knew, too, that the man who gave them to me got them back again before they were warm in my pocket. This thought embittered me, and, picking up the coat, I walked out and stood on the platform of the baggage car. At the next stop they took me off and turned me over to the city marshal,—for the coat belonged to the Superintendent.

"It is like mine, except that it is real, and mine, of course, was only a good imitation. Take it away, wife—do take it away—it haunts me!"

Pitying him, the wife put the coat out of his sight; and immediately he grew calm, drank freely of the strong coffee, but he could not eat. Presently he went over and began to arrange the little Christmas tree in the box his wife had prepared for it during his absence. She began opening the parcels, and when she could trust herself, began to talk about the surprise they would have for the children, and now and again to express her appreciation of some dainty trifle he had selected for her. She watched him closely, noting that his hand was unsteady, and that he was inclined to stagger after stooping for a little while. Finally, when the tree had been trimmed, and the sled for the boy and the doll-carriage for the girl were placed beneath it, she got him to lie down. When she had made him comfortable she kissed him again, knelt by his bed and prayed, or rather offered thanks, and he was asleep.

Two hours later the subdued shouts of her babies, the exclamations of glad surprise that came in stage whispers from the dining-room, woke her, and she rose from the little couch where she had fallen asleep, already dressed to begin the day.

It was four o'clock in the afternoon when she called the prodigal. When he had bathed his feverish face and put on the fresh clothes she had brought in for him and come into the dining-room, he saw his rosy dreams of the previous night fulfilled. The messenger and his wife shook hands with him and wished him a Merry Christmas. His children, all the children, came and kissed him. His wife was smiling, and the warm blood leaping from her happy heart actually put color in her cheeks.

As Downs took the chair at the head of the table he bowed his head, the rest did likewise, and he gave thanks, fervently and without embarrassment.

THE STUFF THAT STANDS

It was very late in the fifties, and Lincoln and Douglas were engaged in animated discussion of the burning questions of the time, when Melvin Jewett journeyed to Bloomington, Illinois, to learn telegraphy.

It was then a new, weird business, and his father advised him not to fool with it. His college chum said to him, as they chatted together for the last time before leaving school, that it would be grewsomely lonely to sit in a dimly lighted flag-station and have that inanimate machine tick off its talk to him in the sable hush of night; but Jewett was ambitious. Being earnest, brave, and industrious, he learned rapidly, and in a few months found himself in charge of a little wooden way-station as agent, operator, yard-master, and everything else. It was lonely, but there was no night work. When the shadows came and hung on the bare walls of his office the spook pictures that had been painted by his school chum, the young operator went over to the little tavern for the night.

True, Springdale at that time was not much of a town; but the telegraph boy had the satisfaction of feeling that he was, by common consent, the biggest man in the place.

Out in a hayfield, he could see from his window a farmer gazing up at the humming wire, and the farmer's boy holding his ear to the pole, trying to understand. All this business that so blinded and bewildered with its mystery, not only the farmer, but the village folks as well, was to him as simple as sunshine.

In a little while he had learned to read a newspaper with one eye and keep the other on the narrow window that looked out along the line; to mark with one ear the "down brakes" signal of the north-bound freight, clear in the siding, and with the other to catch the whistle of the oncoming "cannon ball," faint and far away.

When Jewett had been at Springdale some six or eight months, another young man dropped from the local one morning, and said, "Wie gehts," and handed him a letter. The letter was from the Superintendent, calling him back to Bloomington to despatch trains. Being the youngest of the despatchers, he had to take the "death trick." The day man used to work from eight o'clock in the morning until four o'clock in the afternoon, the "split trick" man from four until midnight, and the "death trick" man from midnight until morning.

We called it the "death trick" because, in the early days of railroading, we had a lot of wrecks about four o'clock in the morning. That was before double tracks and safety inventions had made travelling by rail safer than sleeping at home, and before trainmen off duty had learned to look not on liquor that was red. Jewett, however, was not long on the night shift. He was a good despatcher,—a bit risky at times, the chief thought, but that was only when he knew his man. He was a rusher and ran trains close, but he was ever watchful and wide awake.

In two years' time he had become chief despatcher. During these years the country, so quiet when he first went to Bloomington, had been torn by the tumult of civil strife.

With war news passing under his eye every day, trains going south with soldiers, and cars coming north with the wounded, it is not remarkable that the fever should get into the young despatcher's blood. He read of the great, sad Lincoln, whom he had seen and heard and known, calling for volunteers, and his blood rushed red and hot through his veins. He talked to the trainmen who came in to register, to enginemen waiting for orders, to yardmen in the yards, and to shopmen after hours; and many of them, catching the contagion, urged him to organize a company, and he did. He continued to work days and to drill his men in the twilight. He would have been up and drilling at dawn if he could have gotten them together. He inspired them with his quiet enthusiasm, held them by personal magnetism, and by unselfish patriotism kindled in the breast of each of his fifty followers a desire to do something for his country. Gradually the railroad, so dear to him, slipped back to second place in the affairs of the earth. His country was first. To be sure, there was no shirking of responsibility at the office, but the business of the company was never allowed to overshadow the cause in which he had silently but heartily enlisted. "Abe" Lincoln was, to his way of reasoning, a bigger man than the President of the Chicago and Alton Railroad—which was something to concede. The country must be cared for first, he argued; for what good would a road be with no country to run through?

All day he would work at the despatcher's office, flagging fast freights and "laying out" local passenger trains, to the end that the soldiers might be hurried south. He would pocket the "cannon ball" and order the "thunderbolt" held at Alton for the soldiers' special. "Take siding at

Sundance for troop train, south-bound," he would flash out, and glory in his power to help the government.

All day he would work and scheme for the company (and the Union), and at night, when the silver moonlight lay on the lot back of the machine shops, he would drill and drill as long as he could hold the men together. They were all stout and fearless young fellows, trained and accustomed to danger by the hazard of their daily toil. They knew something of discipline, were used to obeying orders, and to reading and remembering regulations made for their guidance; and Jewett reasoned that they would become, in time, a crack company, and a credit to the state.

By the time he had his company properly drilled, young Jewett was so perfectly saturated with the subject of war that he was almost unfit for duty as a despatcher. Only his anxiety about south-bound troop trains held his mind to the matter and his hand to the wheel. At night, after a long evening in the drill field, he would dream of great battles, and hear in his dreams the ceaseless tramp, tramp of soldiers marching down from the north to reenforce the fellows in the fight.

Finally, when he felt that they were fit, he called his company together for the election of officers. Jewett was the unanimous choice for captain, other officers were chosen, and the captain at once applied for a commission.

The Jewetts were an influential family, and no one doubted the result of the young despatcher's request. He waited anxiously for some time, wrote a second letter, and waited again. "Any news from Springfield?" the conductor would ask, leaving the register, and the chief despatcher would shake his head.

One morning, on entering his office, Jewett found a letter on his desk. It was from the Superintendent, and it stated bluntly that the resignation of the chief despatcher would be accepted, and named his successor.

Jewett read it over a second time, then turned and carried it into the office of his chief.

"Why?" echoed the Superintendent; "you ought to know why. For months you have neglected your office, and have worked and schemed and conspired to get trainmen and enginemen to quit work and go to war. Every day women who are not ready to be widowed come here and cry on the carpet because their husbands are going away with 'Captain' Jewett's company. Only yesterday a schoolgirl came running after me, begging me not to let her little brother, the red-headed peanut on the local, go as drummer-boy in 'Captain' Jewett's company.

"And now, after demoralizing the service and almost breaking up a half a hundred homes, you ask, 'Why?' Is that all you have to say?"

"No," said the despatcher, lifting his head; "I have to say to you, sir, that I have never knowingly neglected my duty. I have not conspired. I have been misjudged and misunderstood; and in conclusion, I would say that my resignation shall be written at once."

Returning to his desk, Jewett found the long-looked-for letter from Springfield. How his heart beat as he broke the seal! How timely—just as things come out in a play. He would not interrupt traffic on the Alton, but with a commission in his pocket would go elsewhere and organize a new company. These things flashed through his mind as he unfolded the letter. His eye fell immediately on the signature at the end. It was not the name of the Governor, who had been a close friend of his father, but of the Lieutenant-Governor. It was a short letter, but plain; and it left no hope. His request had been denied.

This time he did not ask why. He knew why, and knew that the influence of a great railway company, with the best of the argument on its side, would outweigh the influence of a train despatcher and his friends.

Reluctantly Jewett took leave of his old associates in the office, went to his room in the hotel, and sat for hours crushed and discouraged. Presently he rose, kicked the kinks out of his trousers, and walked out into the clear sunlight. At the end of the street he stepped from the side-walk to the sod path and kept walking. He passed an orchard and plucked a ripe peach from an overhanging bough. A yellow-breasted lark stood in a stubble-field, chirped two or three times, and soared, singing, toward the far blue sky. A bare-armed man, with a muley cradle, was cradling grain, and, far away, he heard the hum of a horse-power threshing machine. It had been months, it seemed years, since he had been in the country, felt its cooling breeze, smelled the fresh breath of the fields, or heard the song of a lark; and it rested and refreshed him.

When young Jewett returned to the town he was himself again. He had been guilty of no wrong, but had been about what seemed to him his duty to his country. Still, remembered with sadness the sharp rebuke of the Superintendent, a feeling intensified by the recollection that it was the same official who had brought him in from Springdale, made a train despatcher out of him, and promoted him as often as he had earned promotion. If he had seemed to be acting in bad faith with the officials of the road, he would make amends. That night he called his company together, told them that he had been unable to secure a commission, stated that he had resigned and was going away, and advised them to disband.

The company forming at Lexington was called "The Farmers," just as the Bloomington company was known as the "Car-hands." "The Farmers" was full, the captain said, when Jewett offered his services. At the last moment one of the boys had "heart failure," and Jewett was taken in his place. His experience with the disbanded "Car-hands" helped him and his company immeasurably. It was only a few days after his departure from Bloomington that he again passed through, a private in "The Farmers."

Once in the South, the Lexington company became a part of the 184th Illinois Infantry, and almost immediately engaged in fighting. Jewett panted to be on the firing-line, but that was not to be. The regiment had just captured an important railway which had to be manned and operated at once. It was the only means of supplying a whole army corps with bacon and beans. The colonel of his company was casting about for railroaders, when he heard of Private Jewett. He was surprised to find, in "The Farmers," a man of such wide experience as a railway official, so well posted on the general situation, and so keenly alive to the importance of the railroad and the necessity of keeping it open. Within a week Jewett had made a reputation. If there had been time to name him, he would doubtless have been called superintendent of transportation; but there was no time to classify those who were working on the road. They called him Jewett. In some way the story of the one-time captain's experience at Bloomington came to the colonel's ears, and he sent for Jewett. As a result of the interview, the young private was taken from the ranks, made a captain, and "assigned to special duty." His special duty was that of General Manager of the M. & L. Railroad, with headquarters in a car.

Jewett called upon the colonel again, uninvited this time, and protested. He wanted to get into the fighting. "Don't worry, my boy," said the good-natured colonel, "I'll take the fight out of you later on; for the present, Captain Jewett, you will continue to run this railroad."

The captain saluted and went about his business.

There had been some fierce fighting at the front, and the Yankees had gotten decidedly the worst of it. Several attempts had been made to rush re-enforcements forward by rail, but with poor success. The pilot engines had all been ditched. As a last desperate chance, Jewett determined to try a "black" train. Two engines were attached to a troop-train, and Jewett seated himself on the pilot of the forward locomotive. The lights were all put out. They were to have no pilot engine, but were to slip past the ambuscade, if possible, and take chances on lifted rails and absent bridges. It was near the end of a dark, rainy night. The train was rolling along at a good freight clip, the engines working as full as might be without throwing fire, when suddenly, from either side of the track, a yellow flame flared out, followed immediately by the awful roar of the muskets from whose black mouths the murderous fire had rushed. The bullets fairly rained on the jackets of the engines, and crashed through the cab windows. The engineer on the head engine was shot from his seat. Jewett, in a hail of lead, climbed over the running-board, pulled wide the throttle, and whistled "off brakes." The driver of the second engine, following his example, opened also, and the train was thus whirled out of range, but not until Jewett had been badly wounded. A second volley rained upon the rearmost cars, but did little damage. The enemy had been completely outwitted. They had mistaken the train for a pilot engine, which they had planned to let pass; after which they were to turn a switch, ditch, and capture the train.

There was great rejoicing in the hungry army at the front that dawn, when the long train laden with soldiers and sandwiches arrived. The colonel was complimented by the corps commander, but he was too big and brave to accept promotion for an achievement in which he had had no part or even faith. He told the truth, the whole truth, and nothing but the truth; and, when it was all over, there was no more "Captain" Jewett. When he came out of the hospital he had the rank of a major, but was still "assigned to special duty."

Major Jewett's work became more important as the great struggle went on. Other lines of railway fell into the hands of the Yankees, and all of them in that division of the army came under his control. They were good for him, for they made him a very busy man and kept him from panting for the firing-line. In conjunction with General D., the famous army engineer, who has since become a noted railroad-builder, he rebuilt and re-equipped wrecked railways, bridged wide rivers, and kept a way open for men and supplies to get to the front.

When at last the little, ragged, but ever-heroic remnant of the Confederate army surrendered, and the worn and weary soldiers set their faces to the north again, Major Jewett's name was known throughout the country.

At the close of the war, in recognition of his ability and great service to the Union, Major Jewett was made a brevet colonel, by which title he is known to almost every railway man in America.

Many opportunities came to Colonel Jewett to enter once more the field in which, since his school days, he had been employed. One by one these offers were put aside. They were too easy. He had been so long in the wreck of things that he felt out of place on a prosperous, well-regulated line. He knew of a little struggling road that ran east from Galena, Illinois. It was called the Galena and something, for Galena was at that time the most prosperous and promising town in the wide, wild West.

He sought and secured service on the Galena line and began anew. The road was one of the oldest and poorest in the state, and one of the very first chartered to build west from Chicago. It was sorely in need of a young, vigorous, and experienced man, and Colonel Jewett's ability was not long in finding recognition. Step by step he climbed the ladder until he reached the General Managership. Here his real work began. Here he had some say, and could talk directly to the President, who was one of the chief owners. He soon convinced the company that to succeed they must have more money, build more, and make business by encouraging settlers to go out and plough and plant and reap and ship. The United States government was aiding in the construction of a railway across the "desert," as the West beyond the Missouri River was then called. Jewett urged his company to push out to the Missouri River and connect with the line to the Pacific, and they pushed.

Ten years from the close of the war Colonel Jewett was at the head of one of the most promising railroads in the country. Prosperity followed peace, the West began to build up, the Pacific Railroad was completed, and the little Galena line, with a new charter and a new name, had become an important link connecting the Atlantic and the Pacific.

For nearly half a century Jewett has been at the front, and has never been defeated. The discredited captain of that promising company of car-boys has become one of our great "captains of industry." He is to-day President of one of the most important railroads in the world, whose black fliers race out nightly over twin paths of steel, threading their way in and out of not less than nine states, with nearly nine thousand miles of main line. He has succeeded beyond his wildest dreams; and his success is due largely to the fact that when, in his youth, he mounted to ride to fame and fortune, he did not allow the first jolt to jar him from the saddle. He is made of the stuff that stands.

THE MILWAUKEE RUN

Henry Hautman was born old. He had the face and figure of a voter at fifteen. His skin did not fit his face,—it wrinkled and resembled a piece of rawhide that had been left out in the rain and sun.

Henry's father was a freighter on the Santa Fé trail when Independence was the back door of civilization, opening on a wilderness. Little Henry used to ride on the high seat with his father, close up to the tail of a Missouri mule, the seventh of a series of eight, including the trailer which his father drove in front of the big wagon. It was the wind of the west that tanned the hide on Henry's face and made him look old before his time.

At night they used to arrange the wagons in a ring, in which the freighters slept.

One night Henry was wakened by the yells of Indians, and saw men fighting. Presently he was swung to the back of a cayuse behind a painted warrior, and as they rode away the boy, looking back, saw the wagons burning and guessed the rest.

Later the lad escaped and made his way to Chicago, where he began his career on the rail, and where this story really begins.

It was extremely difficult, in the early days, to find sober, reliable young men to man the few locomotives in America and run the trains. A large part of the population seemed to be floating, drifting west, west, always west. So when this stout-shouldered, strong-faced youth asked for work, the round-house foreman took him on gladly. Henry's boyhood had been so full of peril that he was absolutely indifferent to danger and a stranger to fear. He was not even afraid of work, and at the end of eighteen months he was marked up for a run. He had passed from the wiping gang to the deck of a passenger engine, and was now ready for the road.

Henry was proud of his rapid promotion, especially this last lift, that would enable him to race in the moonlight along the steel trail, though he recalled that it had cost him his first little white lie.

One of the rules of the road said a man must be twenty-one years old before he could handle a locomotive. Henry knew his book well, but he knew also that the railroad needed his service and that he needed the job; so when the clerk had taken his "Personal Record,"—which was only a mild way of asking where he would have his body sent in case he met the fate so common at that time on a new line in a new country,—he gave his age as twenty, hoping the master-mechanic would allow him a year for good behavior.

Years passed. So did the Indian and the buffalo. The railway reached out across the Great American Desert. The border became blurred and was rubbed out. The desert was dotted with homes. Towns began to grow up about the water-tanks and to bud and blow on the treeless plain.

Henry Hautman became known as the coolest and most daring driver on the road. He was a good engineer and a good citizen. He owned his home; and while his pay was not what an engineer draws to-day for the same run made in half the time, it was sufficient unto the day, his requirements, and his wife's taste.

Only one thing troubled him. He had bought a big farm not far from Chicago, for which he was paying out of his savings. If he kept well, as he had done all his life, three years more on the Limited would let him out. Then he could retire a year ahead of time, and settle down in comfort on the farm and watch the trains go by.

It would be his salvation, this farm by the roadside; for the very thought of surrendering the "La Salle" to another was wormwood and gall to Henry. It never occurred to him to quit and go over to the N.W. or the P.D. & Q., where they had no age limit for engineers. No man ever thought of leaving the service of the Chicago, Milwaukee & Wildwood. The road was one of the finest, and as for the run,—well, they used to say, "Drive the Wildwood Limited and die." Henry had driven it for a decade and had not died. When he looked himself over he declared he was the best man, physically, on the line. But there was the law in the Book of Rules,—the Bible of the C.M. & W.,—and no man might go beyond the limit set for the retirement of engine-drivers; and Henry Hautman, the favorite of the "old man," would take his medicine. They were a loyal lot on the Milwaukee in those days. Superintendent Van Law declared them clannish. "Kick a man," said he, "in St. Paul, and his friends will feel the shock in the lower Mississippi."

Time winged on, and as often as Christmas came it reminded the old engineer that he was one year nearer his last trip; for his mother, now sleeping in the far West, had taught him to believe that he had come to her on Christmas Eve.

How the world had aged in threescore years! Sometimes at night he had wild dreams of his last day on the freight wagon, of the endless reaches of waving wild grass, of bands of buffalo racing away toward the setting sun, a wild deer drinking at a running stream, and one lone Indian on the crest of a distant dune, dark, ominous, awful. Sometimes, from his high seat at the front of the Limited, he caught the flash of a field fire and remembered the burning wagons in the wilderness.

But the wilderness was no more, and Henry knew that the world's greatest civilizer, the locomotive, had been the pioneer in all this great work of peopling the plains. The pathfinders, the real heroes of the Anglo-Saxon race, had fought their way from the Missouri River to the sundown sea. He recalled how they used to watch for the one opposing passenger train. Now they flashed by his window as the mile-posts flashed in the early days, for the line had been double-tracked so that the electric-lighted hotels on wheels passed up and down regardless of opposing trains. All these changes had been wrought in a single generation; and Henry felt that he had contributed, according to his light, to the great work.

But the more he pondered the perfection of the service, the comfort of travel, the magnificence of the Wildwood Limited, the more he dreaded the day when he must take his little personal effects from the cab of the La Salle and say good-bye to her, to the road, and hardest of all, to the "old man," as they called the master-mechanic.

One day when Henry was registering in the round-house, he saw a letter in the rack for him, and carried it home to read after supper.

When he read it, he jumped out of his chair. "Why, Henry!" said his wife, putting down her knitting, "what ever's the matter,—open switch or red light?"

"Worse, Mary; it's the end of the track."

The old engineer tossed the letter over to his wife, sat down, stretched his legs out, locked his fingers, and began rolling his thumbs one over the other, staring at the stove.

When Mrs. Hautman had finished the letter she stamped her foot and declared it an outrage. She suggested that somebody wanted the La Salle. "Well," she said, resigning herself to her fate, "I bet I have that coach-seat out of the cab,—it'll make a nice tête-à-tête for the front room. Superannuated!" she went on with growing disgust. "I bet you can put any man on the first division down three times in five."

"It's me that's down, Mary,—down and out."

"Henry Hautman, I'm ashamed of you! you know you've got four years come Christmas—why don't you fight? Where's your Brotherhood you've been paying money to for twenty years? I bet a 'Q' striker comes and takes your engine."

"No, Mary, we're beaten. I see how it all happened now. You see I began at twenty when I was really but sixteen; that's where I lose. I lied to the 'old man' when we were both boys; now that lie comes back to me, as a chicken comes home to roost."

"But can't you explain that now?"

"Well, not easy. It's down in the records—it's Scripture now, as the 'old man' would say. No, the best I can do is to take my medicine like a man; I've got a month yet to think it over."

After that they sat in silence, this childless couple, trying to fashion to themselves how it would seem to be superannuated.

The short December days were all too short for Henry. He counted the hours, marked the movements of the minute-hand on the face of his cab clock, and measured the miles he would have, not to "do" but to enjoy, before Christmas. As the weeks went by the old engineer became a changed man. He had always been cheerful, happy, and good-natured. Now he became thoughtful, silent, melancholy. There was not a man on the first division but grieved because he was going, but no man would dare say so to Henry. Sympathy is about the hardest thing a stout heart ever has to endure.

While Henry was out on his last trip his wife waited upon the master-mechanic and asked him to bring his wife over and spend Christmas Eve with Henry and help her to cheer him up; and the "old man" promised to call that evening.

Although there were half-a-dozen palms itching for the throttle of the La Salle, no man had yet been assigned to the run. And the same kindly feeling of sympathy that prompted this delay prevented the aspirants from pressing their claims. Once, in the lodge room, a young member eager for a regular run opened the question, but saw his mistake when the older members began to hiss like geese, while the Worthy Master smote the table with his maul. Henry saw the La Salle cross the turn-table and back into the round-house, and while he "looked her over," examining every link and pin, each lever and link-lifter, the others hurried away; for it was Christmas Eve, and nobody cared to say good-bye to the old engineer.

When he had walked around her half-a-dozen times, touching her burnished mainpins with the back of his hand, he climbed into the cab and began to gather up his trinkets, his comb and tooth-brush, a small steel monkey-wrench, and a slender brass torch that had been given to him by a friend. Then he sat upon the soft cushioned coach-seat that his wife had coveted, and looked along the hand-railing. He leaned from the cab window and glanced along the twin stubs of steel that passed through the open door and stopped short at the pit, symbolizing the end of his run on the rail. The old boss wiper came with his crew to clean the La Salle, but when he saw the driver there in the cab he passed him by.

Long he sat in silence, having a last visit with La Salle, her brass bands gleaming in the twilight. For years she had carried him safely through snow and sleet and rain, often from dawn till dusk, and sometimes from dusk till dawn again. She had been his life's companion while on the road, who now, "like some familiar face at parting, gained a graver grace."

Presently the lamp-lighters came and began lighting the oil lamps that stood in brackets along the wall; but before their gleam reached his face the old engineer slid down and hurried away home with never a backward glance.

That night when Mrs. Hautman had passed the popcorn and red apples, and they had all eaten and the men had lighted cigars, the engineer's wife brought a worn Bible out and drew a chair near the master-mechanic. The "old man," as he was called, looked at the book, then at the woman, who held it open on her lap.

"Do you believe this book?" she asked earnestly.

"Absolutely," he answered.

"All that is written here?"

"All," said the man.

Then she turned to the fly-leaf and read the record of Henry's birth,—the day, the month, and the year.

Henry came and looked at the book and the faded handwriting, trying to remember; but it was too far away.

The old Bible had been discovered that day deep down in a trunk of old trinkets that had been sent to Henry when his mother died, years ago.

The old engineer took the book and held it on his knees, turned its limp leaves, and dropped upon them the tribute of a strong man's tear.

The "old man" called for the letter he had written, erased the date, set it forward four years, and handed it back to Henry.

"Here, Hank," said he, "here's a Christmas gift for you."

So when the Wildwood Limited was limbered up that Christmas morning, Henry leaned from the window, leaned back, tugged at the throttle again, smiled over at the fireman, and said, "Now, Billy, watch her swallow that cold, stiff steel at about a mile a minute."

Printed by Amazon Italia Logistica S.r.l.
Torrazza Piemonte (TO), Italy